D1498172

RACING TO LOVE

RACING TO LOVE

•

MARTHA AMBROSE

E6F 24100

AVALON BOOKS
THOMAS BOUREGY AND COMPANY, INC.
401 LAFAYETTE STREET
NEW YORK, NEW YORK 10003

PRINTED IN THE UNITED STATES OF AMERICA
ON ACID-FREE PAPER
BY HADDON CRAFTSMEN, SCRANTON, PENNSYLVANIA

RACING TO LOVE

Chapter One

The intense quiet around Tracey Danvers was almost unnatural.

A deserted racetrack was like an engine, she thought as she looked around the Daytona International Raceway. An engine just waiting to be revved up and shoved into gear. It needed the roaring crowds, standing and cheering their favorite drivers; it needed the smell of oil and fuel and fumes as the cars sped past the stands; and most of all it needed her own sleek silver Thunderbird in the lead, guided by her own sure hand.

Tracey's mouth curved into a slow triumphant smile as she imagined herself weaving in and out among the other cars, each one at a speed of almost two hundred miles per hour. She would smoothly, effortlessly take control of the track—and the Daytona 500 would be hers. She wasn't the first woman in racing, but she'd be the one the fans would remember.

The dream she had been waiting a lifetime to achieve was almost within her grasp.

"Give it a run. We'll see how it holds the track," said a voice from the pit area.

Tracey turned abruptly to see a tall, wide-shouldered man wearing a white racing suit climb into a Grand

1

Prix stock car. One of his pit crew was with him, holding a stopwatch in his hand.

"I want to time at least ten laps, Rick," the man with the watch said.

As Tracey watched the cobalt blue car scramble to the center of the track, she noted something familiar about the way the man drove. He moved out aggressively into the middle of the straightaway, holding the car down with just the right amount of speed. He balanced the car as it sped around the embankments. Speed and skill. He had them both. Only the fourth turn did he take too high, and that added precious seconds to his time. Who was he? His face had been hidden by his helmet. But there was something about him. . . . One way to find out, Tracey decided, as she walked over to the pit area, never taking her eyes off the blue car speeding around the track.

"So who's your guy?" she asked as the car raced past them.

"The next winner of the Daytona 500." The man kept his head down, his eyes riveted to the stopwatch.

"Really? Not with those times," Tracey challenged playfully as she peered over his shoulder at the watch.

The man clicked the watch off sharply, his eyes now on the car. "And what makes you an expert?"

She shrugged. "I've seen a few races."

He gave an exasperated snort and ran an impatient hand through his sandy hair. "Right. You and everybody else. Look, why don't you—" He broke off as he turned around and caught sight of Tracey's flaming red hair and wide-set green eyes.

"Mind my own business?" she finished his sentence.

"Yeah. I mean . . . at least I wouldn't like you to feel like you have to. . . . " He shook his head with a rueful grin. "What I meant to say is maybe you don't know much about, you know, racing."

Tracey gave a wry grimace. Typical. Men never expected women to know anything about stock cars. "Maybe I know more about racing than you think."

His look was skeptical.

"In fact, I could give you and your driver some advice if you want." She paused, waiting for his reaction.

The man managed a choking laugh. "Honey, Rick Masters doesn't need any advice on driving—except from me. He wrote the rules."

Tracey couldn't help widening her eyes in surprise. Rick Masters! She had heard about his winning streak last year and there were rumors that he was going to race in Daytona, but she had thought they were just that—rumors. Yet his very presence on the track today seemed to be proof that he was planning to take on the Daytona 500.

"Rules change." Tracey couldn't help ribbing him lightly under her breath as Rick Masters brought the stock car to a sudden halt in front of them.

Rick curled his hands around the top of the window opening and slid out of the car with practised ease. The other man tossed the stopwatch to him. "They're not bad times, Rick."

Rick pulled off his helmet and protective goggles

and looked down at the watch, his face drawn tight in annoyance. "Not great, either. I couldn't—" he broke off as he caught sight of Tracey. "I thought the track was closed today."

Her gaze followed the thin scar that ran from his right temple to his jaw. A pang of compassion shot through her. "As far as I know, this is a public place."

"The little lady has an offer you can't refuse," the other man joked.

Rick's grey eyes regarded her quizzically for a moment. Who was she? "I often refuse offers I can't refuse."

"Even before you hear them?" Tracey countered. He thinks I'm some kind of track groupie, she thought. Those featherlike laugh lines that crinkled around his steel grey eyes were attractive, she realized.

"Okay. What's your proposition?" Rick emphasized the last word tiredly. He had a long day ahead of him and no time for games. Still, the challenge in her voice piqued his curiosity.

Spurred on to snap him out of his weariness, Tracey slowly reached out and grasped his roughened hand with her own slim one. His fingers were slim and strong; the hands of a born driver, they radiated power and control. "Only this. . . . " She lifted the watch out of his hand. "You could improve your timing at least five seconds per lap by not taking turn four so high on the embankment." She dangled the watch in front of his startled eyes.

"Huh?" Rick snatched the offensive timepiece out of Tracey's hands.

"That's my offer—advice. No charge."

"Free?" Rick played along. He was intrigued. She was just about the most unexpected thing to breeze into his life in a long while. And how did she know so much about racing?

"Yes. You don't have a thing I'd want in return."

This time Rick couldn't help laughing at her audacity. Her face was a little too angular; her mouth a little too thin. But she had spirit and fire. Even her red hair radiated vitality. And suddenly what seemed to be just another day of work and practice became filled with the promise of something new and exciting.

"Sometimes the best things in life *are* free," Rick agreed.

"And sometimes the best costs the most—in racing that is," the other man said with a slight edge to his voice.

Rick gave a short laugh. "There speaks my crew chief and penny-counting manager—Skid Parker."

Skid extended a hand to Tracey. "And you are . . . ?"

"An anonymous fan . . . of racing," she replied evasively as she shook the offered hand. No need to reveal her identity. This was too much fun. Besides, as she well knew, that glint of interest in Rick's eyes might disappear if he knew she was a competitor.

"Well, Miss Anonymous Fan." Rick leaned back against his car, his helmet under his arm. His eyes flickered appreciatively as they took in her figure nicely featured in her red plaid shirt and jeans. "How did you learn so much about NASCAR?"

"About what?"

"NASCAR. You know: National Association for Stock Car Auto Racing," Skid answered patiently. He then proceeded to explain about the series of races that occurred all year within the division, and how drivers added up points from each win toward the greatest honor: the Winston Cup trophy.

Rick felt a smile tug at his mouth as he listened to Skid trying to impress the girl. Her smiling, friendly face took in everything Skid was saying, but Rick sensed she was leading both of them on—not that he minded. He could stand to look at those deep, green eyes all day.

"I think she knows something about stock car racing," Rick finally interrupted Skid and cut off his own beach fantasy.

Tracey gave a sheepish smile to both men. "Guilty. My brother's mad about racing. He's taken me to a lot of events."

"Does he race?" Rick asked.

"Not really . . . he likes to work in the pit. He prefers the mechanics of racing more than the actual driving. He says driving takes more of a commitment than he's willing to give." She wasn't lying. Her twin, Troy, did want to be a crew chief; he just happened to be *her* crew chief.

Rick looked down at his helmet for a few seconds. Frowning, he brushed his thumb over the long scratches that marred the head gear. Would he ever be able to forget about the accident? The sounds of crashing metal. He shook his head slightly before he looked up again and continued, ''There's no doubt about the commitment. Racing has a way of taking hold of your life from morning till night. You sleep, eat and dream about being in that car.''

''I know what you mean,'' Tracey let slip out before she could stop herself. ''At least . . . that's what my brother tells me.''

''I'd like to meet him. If he's looking for a job, I can use a good mechanic,'' Rick offered, oblivious to the surprised look on Skid's face. Maybe the brother would be a way to get to know her better. And he could use another mechanic. But, Rick was finding it difficult to think about her brother at all, when he looked down into her vividly excited face. ''And all the free advice you'd care to offer,'' he couldn't resist adding.

''Thanks. I'll pass it on to him.'' Tracey found herself drawn to this tall, serious-looking man. Most grey eyes had a cold and forbidding look, but his were as warm as aged pewter. Watch it, she warned herself. She'd felt that way only once before—and it hadn't worked out. She'd been too trusting and she'd let herself in for heartache.

But Rick Masters might be different, a tiny voice whispered inside. In spite of his black hair falling over his forehead and a slight stubble across the lower part of his face, Rick wasn't the rough sort that she usually met in stock car racing. He had style and intelligence. Hard-won integrity was stamped in the rugged planes of his face. Definitely a winner.

Skid reached over and took the stopwatch from Rick.

He looked at the times and then at Tracey. "You'd better leave racing to the professionals."

"I'll try," she answered with mock humility, trying to shake the enveloping presence of Rick Masters. "Maybe I'll come and watch you race sometime."

Rick gave her a long stare as if he couldn't quite figure her out. "Anytime. But you have to promise not to interfere with my concentration."

"You've got it," Tracey tossed off as she swiveled slowly, her delight growing. In spite of the caution bells going off in her mind, she felt positively light-headed. Before she was quite out of earshot, she heard Skid say: "You know, Rick, she might have something there about that fourth turn. . . . "

But Rick wasn't listening. He was still watching Tracey's retreating figure. Her red hair gleamed with gold lights under the hot Florida sun. For a moment, he had an impulse to run after her and beg for her name and phone number. He couldn't let her get away without knowing at least who she was. She'd been an island of enchantment in an otherwise annoying and thoroughly frustrating day.

But something held him back as he watched her disappear behind the stands. He had work to do and no time to dream of red-haired lovelies, even if they did share his interest in racing. Almost throwing his helmet down in disgust, he asked himself why had he let himself get caught up in racing again. It was all Skid's fault.

Rick had been successfully designing engines in California for a large auto company and was experimenting with a new design when this bulldogged, fast-talking guy introduced himself as Skid Parker. Skid said he had recognized Rick in a local newspaper article and proposed that he start racing again, with Skid himself as his manager and crew chief—taking a substantial cut of the profit, of course.

Rick had initially laughed off the proposal, but it set him to thinking about professional racing again. He had to admit to himself that he'd never gotten it out of his system and, for some time, he'd been feeling restless for the challenge and speed of being in a high-powered set of wheels. After eight years of avoiding the sport and making himself one of the most respected engine designers, eventually buying into the company he worked for, he realized he still wanted to prove something on the track, something he wasn't even quite sure of himself.

So six months ago, Rick sold his share of the company and slipped back into stock car racing again.

But it was a slow process to get his driving skills back again—slow and frustrating. Not to mention the continual battle with his old ghosts.

Almost involuntarily, his glance drifted over to the fourth turn of the raceway. How many times had he relived that memory. . . .

The right front tire blew out, jerking the speeding car hard to the right. Rick struggled with the wheel while working the brake pedal, but the strength in his arms was no match for the force of the momentum. The car spun out of control, throwing the front end against the wall of the racetrack with a sickening

Racing to Love

*crunch of metal. His neck snapped back at the moment
of impact and he lost consciousness for a split second.
Then the front windshield kicked out and he watched
the world turn crazily as the car rolled over and over.
The jarring sounds of ripping metal filled his ears, as
the stench of burning oil and rubber filled the air. Then
the awful silence, the searing pain—*

"Earth calling Rick Masters. Earth calling Rick
Masters."

"Sorry, Skid. I was spacing out."

"No problem." Skid clicked the buttons on the stopwatch to set it again. "I want to time a few more laps."

Rick nodded in grim agreement.

"That's him. Rick Masters ten years ago. But he
could be one of your strongest competitors today,"
James Danvers commented in the darkness as a picture
of a younger, leaner Rick in a heavily padded racing
suit flickered across the screen.

Tracey watched the cocky young man flash a wide
grin and give the thumbs-up sign as he climbed into
his old model stock car. Then he quickly maneuvered
into the starting line. She watched even more closely
as the film cut to footage of him during the race. He
took the turns expertly, but with more speed than he
really needed. In the straightaway, he passed cars by
letting his car get caught in the draft-pull behind them;
then he shot around the surprised drivers before the
next turn. She was amazed at the chances he took. At
one point, she caught her breath as Rick almost grazed
the side of the car to the left of him, but he pulled out
in front just in time to avoid a collision. He had nerves

of steel, she thought as she observed him take one obstacle after another, easing up on his speed only when it was absolutely necessary. But he took too many risks.

"God, I can't believe how he took command of the entire track," Troy exclaimed to his father and twin sister.

"Don't forget it either, Troy," his father said sternly as he switched off the film projector. Then he limped across the hardwood floor to turn on the lights. The comfortable den with its high beamed ceilings and sand-colored walls was suddenly illuminated. He blinked for a moment until his eyes cleared from the abrupt shift from darkness to light. As he came back to join them, Tracey noted that his weak leg had stiffened because he had been sitting for so long watching the film.

"Dad," Tracey began thoughtfully, "did you ever race against him?"

Her father shook his head as a half smile crossed his face. His racing days were still fondly remembered even though they had almost cost him his life. As it was, the limp in his right leg was a constant reminder of the dangers of racing. But racing hadn't taken its toll on his looks. He was an impressive man in his fifties who was still handsome even with the grey streaks in his black hair. "No, Tracey . . . at least, I don't think so. I was just about ready to retire when Rick Masters started racing in his early twenties. Then he quit after only a few years."

"And now he's back again." Tracey settled comfortably into the soft beige leather chair as she chewed on a piece of her favorite candy: chocolate-coated almonds. "Hmm. That would make him about—"

"Mid-thirties," Troy cut in absently as he finished his sister's sentence for her. He grabbed a piece of chocolate out of her hand and popped it into his own mouth. "You've had enough."

"I think better when I'm eating chocolate." Tracey defiantly took another piece and savored each bite. "But, Dad, why did Rick Masters quit?"

"No one knows."

"Sponsorship?" Troy offered.

"He had it—some of the biggest companies backed him. Then he had a crash up at Daytona—a big one. It took him out of racing for a while and he never came back."

"Lost his nerve?" Troy questioned.

James shook his head. "I don't think so. He didn't seem like the type to give it up because of a crash, however bad it was. I could be wrong, but it just doesn't figure." James helped himself to a piece of chocolate, acknowledging the family weakness. "At any rate, he dropped out of the racing circuit overnight and started designing engines for a company out west. No explanation, no contact with anybody from his racing days. Then, out of the blue last year, he started racing again with enough money to co-sponsor his own car."

"What's more, the mysterious Mr. Masters is winning again," Tracey commented, trying to keep her voice matter-of-fact. She wanted to know every scrap of information about the man she had met this morning.

"Right. He's in his prime, a seasoned driver, even though he's been out of it for a while. And a real threat to your winning your first big race, Tracey," James reminded her. "It was a good idea to suggest watching the old footage of Rick. You want to get a feel for the way your competition drives."

Tracey smiled weakly.

"What about Carrera and Fielding?" Troy asked. "They're two of the all-time point winners in NAS-CAR. Aren't they just as much competition to us?"

"I don't think so. They've both had a run of bad luck the last two years. Paco Carrera's had a lot of minor accidents, so he's having problems getting sponsorship. And Fielding just isn't racing well. He's taking too many chances. Also, neither of them paces himself on the track. They start out fast, very fast, but then can't keep it up and start to fade."

"So that's why they've been driving in some of the smaller races—to still build points toward the Winston Cup," Tracey said absently.

Her mind wandered away from what her father and brother were saying; she was thinking about Rick Masters. In fact, she'd hardly been able to think about anything else. However foolhardy he was on the track before, he now had the maturity to be a great driver. He wasn't an inexperienced young man using speed for a thrill. He had the intense, controlled determination to win big time. Like her father said, he was going to be their greatest competition.

In fact, there seemed little trace of the immature young Rick Masters in the man she'd met today. He was a man pursuing a single goal—to win. Whatever happened after his crash years ago, there was little to fault in his driving today, except for the high fourth turn. She smiled a little as she remembered his reaction to her advice. Then she suddenly had a mental image of his face smiling down at her as she dangled the stopwatch in front of him. He had taken her teasing in good humor. There was warmth and honesty—Stop, she told herself. She couldn't afford to make a mistake like she had before.

"Tracey!" her father broke into her thoughts. "Did you hear what I said about those modifications on your engine?"

She offered an apologetic smile. "Sorry, Dad."

Troy shook his head impatiently. "He was describing the engine changes in your Thunderbird. If we can raise the horsepower when the restrictor plates are installed, we'll be able to get even greater speed out of it."

Tracey pushed the image of Rick Masters to the back of her mind as she gave her attention once more to her father and brother. She wanted to keep her meeting with Rick to herself. She'd already made a fool of herself once over a guy who was a racer. Her mind bitterly spewed out the name of Roger Harmon. She had met him three years ago when she was breaking into racing at the Carolina dirt tracks. Tracey thought it was love. He wanted to trade on the Danvers name. Unfeminine, Roger called her—especially when she started to beat him. Eventually, he cut out of racing when he couldn't make the grade—after he'd already broken off his relationship with her.

Anyway, Rick was just another driver. What did it matter if he did have the most intriguing amber flecks in his grey eyes? She would be meeting him only professionally.

James Danvers could barely hold back the excitement in his voice. "You'll be able to hit the highest speeds without a bit of a vibration, and—"

"Just what's going on in here?" Mrs. Carleton, their housekeeper inquired in a brusque tone. "As if I had to ask."

Tracey turned around to see the large-boned woman march into the room.

Before she could answer, Troy cut in with feigned innocence. "We're just watching old films, Carley."

Mrs. Carleton raised her brows in disbelief. "Really? Probably more of that racing nonsense."

Tracey cleared her throat dramatically. She'd be the one to take the plunge and confess. "You've caught us, again. It's true. We're watching old racing footage."

"As if I didn't know." She sniffed. "It's not right to be turning a young lady into one of those high speed drivers. It just isn't the thing for her to be doing— hardly a sport for women."

"Now, Mrs. Carleton—" James began.

"As if driving on those dirty tracks and working on those smelly engines isn't enough," she continued, ignoring her employer. "Now you've got Tracey gal-

livanting off on some three-day race all over the state
with all those rough and rowdy men.''

Tracey smiled indulgently. ''It's the All-Florida
Pace-car Rally. And I'll be driving with Troy.''

''That's right,'' Troy added. ''It's just for publicity
before the Daytona—nothing dangerous or risky.''

''Hah! Daytona! A pretty girl like Tracey, at twenty-
five risking her life—and for what?'' Mrs. Carleton
leveled her gaze at James.

Tracey restrained a laugh as she watched her father
roll his eyes upwards in supplication. Mrs. Carleton
had been their housekeeper since Tracey was a little
girl and she had never made a secret of her disapproval
of Tracey's career choice.

''You know it's what Tracey wants. She and Troy
are a winning pair if I've ever seen one. They'll set
the racing world on fire.'' James couldn't help the note
of pride that always crept into his voice.

''And how could she want any different? Growing
up with only men in this house?'' Mrs. Carleton answered indignantly.

Tracey shot a glance at her father in time to see a
shadow of pain cross his face. She knew he still
mourned the loss of her mother—a mother she didn't
even remember.

Mrs. Carleton eyes flickered over Tracey critically.
''It just isn't right.''

''But it's my dream, too,'' Tracey answered quietly.
My dream and *his* dream, she thought as the image of
Rick Masters rose in her mind. But only one could
win.

Chapter Two

"Jake! Jake!" A deep voice reverberated through the garage.

"He's—" Tracey started to shout from where she was positioned on a dolly under her car. But she halted when she heard another male voice ask somewhat sarcastically, "Look, what do you think this little operation can do for you?"

" 'Little garage' is hardly what I'd call Jake's place. He may not have a big operation like some of the other guys, but he's the best in the business."

Tracey detected the impatience in his voice. Whoever the man was, at least he knew a good mechanic from a bad one. She started to slide the dolly out from under the car when the other man continued.

"You know, Rick, this guy works closely with the Danvers team. How can you be certain that you can trust him?"

Tracey froze where she was under the car. Rick Masters. A wave of awareness washed over her at the sound of his deep-timbred voice. But why was he here now, only a month before the Daytona 500? His car seemed to be running fine yesterday and, if he did have problems, surely his own pit crew could handle it. She tried to angle her head from under the car to see the two men. It was impossible. The dolly made it difficult for her to even lift her head slightly. Then she stopped trying altogether as she heard the two men's footsteps growing closer.

Rick continued with cool authority, though still somewhat impatient. "If you're questioning Jake's integrity, you're off target, Skid. The guy's reputation is spotless. A lot of the racers use him. And as for the Danvers team. . . . "

He paused for a few seconds, and Tracey strained her ears to hear what he was saying.

"They're welcome to use the same facilities. There's no place for pettiness in this profession."

"Pettiness, no. A little discretion, yes. Do you want the whole world to know you're having engine problems?"

"So what else is new? Who doesn't have engine problems?" Rick spoke with calm assurance.

Tracey started to nod in agreement but was stopped short as she hit her forehead on the chassis.

"Yeah, well, I don't see any real competition there. Probably some rich kids looking for cheap thrills," Skid scoffed.

"Wait a minute—"

"Women just don't have what it takes to drive competitively," Skid continued. "The strain, the pressure. It's bad enough on men, but women are only asking for trouble when they get behind the wheel of a high-powered engine. Even you felt the pressure along those steep banks at Bristol last year. Remember how your neck muscles locked after only 100 laps?''

''It felt like a knife going through my neck. It's true. I can't see a woman coping with that.''

''Exactly what I mean.'' There seemed to be a note of self-satisfaction in Skid's voice. ''That's why no woman is going to be any kind of challenge to you. I doubt if this Danvers girl could last more than fifty laps, max. You'll blow her away.''

Feeling the dangerous level of her own anger, Tracey had to bite her tongue so as not to let out a sound. But as she tensed to keep quiet, she dropped her wrench. The socket wrench made a distinct clang on the rough, concrete floor, and then slid out past the front tire.

''What was that?'' Skid asked as he turned in the direction of the sound.

The two men walked over to investigate and found where Tracey was still positioned under the car. All they could see, though, were two white overall-clad legs and safety booted feet.

''Hey, buddy, is Jake around?'' Rick Masters asked, obviously taking her for one of the guys who worked on cars in the garage.

Tracey just lay there, knowing if she answered, they would realize she was a woman. She didn't want to have to face Rick Masters looking the way she did. It still hurt to remember how Roger had always called her unfeminine because she worked on her own engines. And she didn't want Rick's grey eyes raking over her, noting the grease on her clothes and her face—perhaps not thinking she was womanly enough because she took on a man's job.

The silence stretched on for a few moments as Tracey cleared her throat nervously; she had to say something. But she didn't want to reveal herself. Her heart started thumping so loudly, she thought surely they could hear it. Just then she detected Jake's heavy steps lumbering into the vicinity, and she gave a silent prayer of thanks.

She had known Jake Williams since she was a child and she trusted him implicitly. He had been part of her father's pit crew when he used to race and, when he retired, Jake opened the garage which was used almost exclusively to test high-powered race car engines. People came from all over the country to consult with Jake, but he contented himself with this small operation in Daytona Beach.

"Jake, you old dog. Still at the engines, I see."

"Hey, good to see you, too, Rick. It's been a long time."

So they knew each other, Tracey realized. She pictured Rick extending his hand, trying not to wince as it was grasped in Jake's massive grip.

"This is my crew chief, Skid Parker."

Tracey hoped these amenities would soon be over, since she was growing impatient lying in her prone position under the car. She also had an absurd desire to kick Skid in the shin.

"Anyone else here when you came in?" Jake asked.

"Just one of your boys." Rick nudged the overall clad legs with his foot. Tracey caught her breath again.

Rick continued quickly, suppressing the odd sensation he'd noted when he lightly kicked the mechanic's leg. "Jake, I need you to look at my Grand Prix. I'm having some problems with the cooling system; the engine keeps heating up too quickly, and then I have to cut back on the speed when I most need it."

"What about your own mechanics?"

"To be honest, they can't figure it out and neither can I. It's my design, but I only design them. I can't fix them."

Jake hesitated. "And you think I can?"

"I know you can."

"Hmm, maybe. But I'm not making any promises." Jake sounded noncommittal, but Tracey could tell from his tone of voice that he was also pleased by the compliment.

Tracey let them talk for a while, carefully listening to the problems Rick Masters was describing. After hearing Skid's chauvinistic comments, she felt almost gleeful that they were having problems with their engine. Rick Masters might have his own large pit crew, but that didn't count for everything.

Then her thoughts turned back to her own car. If I don't get back to work, I'm not going to have it ready for the Daytona, she thought. Her hand inched over to where the wrench had fallen, but she couldn't reach it without her hand being in full view of the men. Darn! She clenched her fist. I've got to get off this wretched dolly.

Just when it seemed as though they were wrapping up their discussion, Tracey heard—

"Hi, Jake! Just came in to see if Tra—" Troy

stopped in the middle of the sentence when he realized that Rick Masters was the man talking to Jake.

"Troy, this is Rick Masters, and his crew chief," Jake interrupted, to Tracey's grateful relief. He must have known that she didn't want her presence known.

"A pleasure to meet you," Troy responded enthusiastically. "I've seen films of your old races."

Rick laughed not unkindly at Troy's youthful exuberance. He remembered what it was like when he was just starting out; all the other drivers seemed like gods—immortal *and* ancient. "Thanks, but you're making me feel like your father. The next thing you'll be telling me is that you grew up watching my races."

"I . . . well. . . . " Troy paused. "So Jake, where is my—" He broke off as Tracey gave him a slight kick in his shins.

"Is something wrong?" Rick asked.

"No, no . . . I was looking for my—uh—engine timing results from the last trial lap." He never was much of a liar, Tracey thought miserably.

"Isn't this yours?" Rick tapped on the hood of the silver car next to them.

Troy shook his head. "No it's my sister's—Tracey's. She's trying to break into the NASCAR circuit and I'm working as her crew chief."

Rick Masters' voice sounded expressionless. "Yes, I'd heard you're entered in the road rally next week as a team. I'm going to run in it myself. She must be pretty good to take on something as rough as a three-day rally from one end of the state to the other."

Tracey wasn't fooled by this compliment. Of course

he wouldn't say anything like she'd just overheard—
he didn't think she was much competition at all.

"She's the best!" Troy exclaimed. "I'll introduce
you if you're going to the Celebrity Car Wash tomorrow."

Oh no. Tracey moaned to herself. She couldn't let
Troy introduce them tomorrow—she'd already met
Rick. How could she explain that? What had possessed
her to tease him like that at the Raceway yesterday?
She didn't know what had gotten into her. But when
Rick had taken off his helmet, a sudden sense of play-
fulness had overcome her. And that smile of his. . . .
She brushed the hair off her damp forehead with the
back of her hand. This was getting worse and worse
by the minute. She could only hope that maybe Rick
would be busy tomorrow.

"I'll be there. I never miss a charity event—especially one for the Children's Foundation." In spite of
what Skid had said, Rick was intrigued with this
woman who might be taking on not only the rally, but
NASCAR itself. She had to be extraordinary even to
try it. Then the image of the red-haired enchantress he
had met yesterday appeared in his mind. She was attractive. She was vivacious. She loved racing. What
more could he ask for? He'd been so mesmerized he
hadn't even asked her for her phone number. He'd
mentally kicked himself a hundred times for that over-
sight.

Can't Troy see that Rick is just scouting out the
competition? Tracey thought in exasperation. Just like
Roger. Those kinds of men acted interested, then they

felt threatened, and finally they'd just walk out when the competition grew too fierce. A tiny voice inside told her that maybe Rick was different—but she immediately smothered it.

Jake made an impatient noise in his throat. "I've got work to do . . . but if you want to bring your car over tomorrow, Rick, I'll look at it."

"Thanks. I wanted you to. . . . " Rick paused as he looked down at the mechanic still positioned under the car. There was something, but—no, it was silly. . . . He shook his head. That woman had really rattled him yesterday. "Right—Jake, my cooling system. . . . " As he was explaining what he wanted Jake to do, Tracey heard their footsteps recede from the garage, and she breathed a sigh of relief.

"Troy! Help me out from under this car!" she snapped at her twin. He pulled the dolly out and helped Tracey to stand up again.

"What in the world were you doing under the car? Why didn't you come out and meet Rick?" Troy asked as he tried to hold Tracey's somewhat unsteady figure.

She took a few deep breaths and flexed her muscles until she felt a tingling sensation in her legs again.

Then she turned on Troy in annoyance. "Come out and meet him?" she imitated her twin sarcastically. "Just look at me! Can you see me offering him my greasy hand when I'm introduced to one of the most famous stock car drivers in the world today? You've got to be kidding."

She tried to straighten her overalls and wipe the grime off her face with the back of her slim hand.

Troy looked at his twin in remorse. "I guess you do look a little disgusting, but I'm sure that someone like Rick Masters would understand since he works on his own cars himself. He isn't a jerk like Roger—"

Tracey's sudden glare silenced her twin. "And, of course, you just had to ask him if he's going to the celebrity event tomorrow."

"Tracey, I don't see what you're getting so steamed up about. We've met most of our other competitors socially at other functions. You can't let—"

"Not Rick Masters! He's not like the rest of them. He's too—" Tracey had to stop herself. She didn't want her twin to realize her interest in Rick was more than professional. Maybe she didn't want to admit it even to herself. "He's too much . . . , well, he's going to be a challenge on the track."

Troy grinned. "That's nothing new for you. You can outdrive most other men, and no one's intimidated you yet."

"I haven't been driving in the big time yet, and— I don't know. Maybe I'm getting too stressed out. I'm going to see if Dad has the engine specs." She shoved her clipboard against her brother's stomach. "Here, you work on the restrictor plates."

"What's the matter with them?"

"They're reducing the speed, and—Oh, never mind, I'll tell you later." She started out the door and then tossed off over her shoulder: "Better yet—have Jake explain it to you. I've got work to do if we're going to win the Daytona."

* * *

Once they arrived at the Oceanview Resort, sponsor
of the Celebrity Car Wash, Tracey scanned the grounds
for Rick Masters.

"Dad, why don't you and Troy join the pit crew?
I'll go stand by my car under the tent and see if any
of the kids want some pictures," she prompted. Rick
might be under the huge green and blue tent that had
been set up for the car exhibitions.

"Oh, sure, stick us with the crew washing cars,
while you pose next to your stock car," Troy drawled.
"And, by the way, why are you wearing a dress?"

Tracey lifted her chin. "I wear them—occasion-
ally."

"Yeah, once a year," Troy added with light sarcasm. Then he peered closer. "And is that make-up
you have on?"

"What if it is?" Tracey asked in a dangerous tone.

"Nothing wrong with dressing up," James interrupted, herding Troy over to the car washing area.

As Tracey entered the tent, she looked down at the
emerald green, sleeveless cotton dress she had slipped
on at the last minute this morning. Was it too much?
She was going to have some publicity photos taken
today and, besides, the salesperson had said it looked
good on her when she tried it on yesterday. And she
had carefully blended the light beige foundation and
sable eye shadow to enhance her "unusual coloring"
as the woman at the department store cosmetic counter
had told her yesterday. The last thing she wanted to
do was face Rick Masters looking like the "grease
monkey" Troy was always calling her.

Her glance swept over the various stockcars and their drivers until she spotted Rick Masters. There he was. She was amazed at the thrill that ran through her, just seeing him again. Tracey took deep, calming breaths as she slowly made her way over to where Rick was standing next to her silver Thunderbird. He was looking at a huge photograph of her father winning his last race. It was a giant blow-up of his car passing the finish line at the Indy 500. Troy had placed it there to show that racing was a Danvers family tradition.

Tracey figured she might as well get it over with and introduce herself—otherwise it could be awkward later with her father and brother present.

Tracey paused, but her movements were heard as Rick Masters turned around to look at her.

"It's the Anonymous Fan," he mocked lightly. "Or should I say, Miss Tracey Danvers?"

Tracey flushed. "Right on both counts."

"I saw you come in with your father and brother," he explained. "The resemblance between you and your brother is incredible."

"Actually, he's my twin."

"So why the deception the other day?"

She shrugged and gave a little laugh. "It seemed like a good idea at the time."

Rick eyes flickered in disbelief.

"Okay. I don't usually tell men that I'm a racecar driver when I first meet them," she admitted. "It seems to put them off." That was an understatement. It was a death knell to a relationship.

"I don't know why." Rick's eyes lingered on her

creamy, lightly tanned shoulders. He couldn't believe his luck that the vibrant woman he met the other day was actually a fellow driver. He hadn't been able to get her out of his thoughts since she'd appeared at the Raceway, and now here she was—turning out to be none other than Tracey Danvers. "So what's a nice girl like you doing in a profession like this?" he asked.

Tracey laughed. "Same as you—pursuing fame and fortune."

"I thought we were trying to break the speed of sound."

"That, too," Tracey agreed, warming to his humor. It was criminal for a man to look as good as he did in a casual shirt and pants. In spite of his scar, his clean-shaven face had a compelling handsomeness. "So you're not intimidated by a woman racing in the car next to you?"

Rick paused. "Intimidated, no. Concerned, maybe."

Tracey bristled slightly, remembering Skid's comments at the garage. "What are you getting at?"

Rick felt caution alerts going off in his mind. He didn't want to blow it with this woman. But the soft sheen of the color of the dress only deepened the green of her eyes, making it almost impossible for him to concentrate on what he was saying. "What I mean is, that the body takes a lot of physical pounding on the race track."

"Don't you think I can hack it?" Tracey challenged, a shade too loudly. She looked around and noticed a few people in the tent had turned to look at them.

"I didn't say that. I don't know, do I?" Rick responded in a low voice.

"No," she said, slightly mollified. He was right; he didn't know how she drove. She was letting her own self-doubt lead her to make snap judgments.

"None of us really knows until we're burning up the track, trying to hold the car down, seeing that wall only inches away." His eyes clouded with visions of past races. He could feel the heat and the dirt and the tension. Then he caught himself and shook his head slightly to bring himself back to reality. "Only you know if you measure up."

"All I know is—there's nothing as exciting as racing." Until I met you, Tracey mentally noted. "It's in my blood. It's what I've always wanted to do."

"Me, too." Rick's eyes glowed with an intensity that matched Tracey's. Just knowing they shared a love for racing made him feel connected to her—and made him wonder what else they had in common. "You never get it out of your system. The fire, the speed—it's always there."

"I'm willing to take on the physical challenge. It's dangerous, but I can handle it."

"Exciting. Crazy. Dangerous. It's all those things, all right. And add one more thing: consuming. It can also consume you," Rick warned, but the last thing he wanted to do was be cautious. Her enthusiasm was contagious. It charged him.

"But what a way to go," Tracey tossed off in her usual offhand manner, yet her flippancy dissolved as she locked eyes with Rick.

The silence stretched on as Rick noticed that the tent seemed empty. Only the two of them stood there in front of the large picture portraying the excitement of winning. Rick was only inches from her, and he could smell the soft gardenia scent of her perfume. It was sweetly feminine. He wanted to reach out and touch a strand of her red hair and see if it was as silky soft as the rest of her appeared to be.

Trying to break the spell, Tracey finally asked, "I guess the job offer for my brother is out, now that you know who I am?"

For a few moments they continued to search each other's eyes. "I can always use . . . uh . . . another mechanic," Rick murmured. He fell silent again.

"Mr. Masters, can I have a picture of you?" A small voice broke into their silent longing.

Tracey and Rick looked down simultaneously at the young boy pulling on Rick's pant leg. His large brown eyes gazed up at Rick with undisguised admiration. "Can I have a picture?" he asked again, holding out his camera.

"I can do better than that," Rick said as he easily swung the boy up in his strong arms.

"Maybe this pretty lady would take a picture of the two of us together by her car," Rick suggested as he handed the camera to Tracey.

"This is *her* car?" the boy asked, his eyes widening in surprise.

"Yup," Rick answered. "She's a race car driver just like me."

Tracey couldn't help the swelling emotion in her

heart. Rick actually sounded proud of her ability to drive as his equal. What a difference from Roger who used to try to shove her in the background as much as possible. ''So what do you think of that?'' Tracey asked the boy as she adjusted the camera setting.

''I think it's great,'' he said enthusiastically.

Tracey and Rick shared a smile. She held the camera up to center Rick and the boy through the lens. And as she brought the two of them into focus, she saw Rick ruffle the boy's hair affectionately. Her heart gave a lurch at genuine emotion on Rick's face. Or was it just pretense for the picture—an act for a young fan?

Tracey quickly snapped a couple of pictures. ''There you go.'' She handed the camera back to the boy.

''Wait a minute.'' Rick set the boy down. Then he took a publicity photograph out of his shirt pocket. ''What's your name, son?''

''Danny.''

''Do you want to drive race cars?'' Rick asked gently, knowing how shy he had felt at that age.

''Boy, do I!'' Danny responded.

''Okay, here you go.'' Rick took a pen and scribbled something on the photograph. ''It says, 'To the next world-famous stock car driver—Danny.' ''

''Thanks,'' Danny said as he held the picture almost reverently.

''You see that guy over there?'' Rick pointed at Skid who was standing next to Rick's car. Danny nodded. ''I want you to tell him I said to give you and your friends passes for the Daytona 500 race. You can come down to the pit before the race. Okay?''

"Great! Thanks, Mr. Masters!"

"Rick." Rick took Danny's small hand in his and shook it. Danny then tore off at a run toward Skid.

"I think you've got a fan for life," Tracey said, trying to hide the emotions that were racing through her with a tone of asperity.

Rick's smile faded a little. "I didn't do it for that reason, Tracey. I like kids—I was an only child, so I know what it's like to feel alone. That's why I come to these events."

"Sorry." Tracey cast her eyes down, not wanting Rick to see the shadows she knew were there. "Most of the men I meet in this profession are—well—out for only themselves."

"That's not me," Rick said with quiet emphasis. He wondered who the guy was who had hurt Tracey— made her so wary. "Since I've gone back into racing, I'm on the road a lot. I can't deny it. But I'd like to have a home base somewhere."

"It goes with the profession—drifting from track to track," she murmured.

"I don't know," Rick challenged. "You seem to have gotten around it."

"Me?" Her startled glance met his calm one.

"Sure. You've got your father and brother. A real family. You live together in Daytona. I envy you that."

Surprise flooded through Tracey. Was Rick trying to tell her he was lonely? "I guess I am lucky to have both a home and the freedom to race." She suddenly pictured the white clapboard house on stilts where she had grown up on Daytona Beach. It was a place of many happy memories. ''Troy and I were practically beach bums—we spent every waking minute as children on the beach.''

''And you had each other,'' Rick reminded her.

''Hey, wait a second. Let me tell you, having a twin can be a real pain sometimes,'' Tracey informed him, but the trace of a smile softened her words.

''How so?'' Rick wanted to see that smile stay on her face.

''Twins can sort of sense each other's emotions— Troy's specialty was always knowing when I was up to something—and, of course, he'd always tell our father.'' Her face brightened in remembrance. ''Dad still thinks I was the most mischievous child going.''

''No,'' Rick scoffed mockingly. ''Not with that sedate hair color of yours.''

''You see? Not only do I have a twin to live down, but this darn hair as well.'' Tracey fell into his light-hearted banter. She didn't know why she was suddenly telling him childhood stories, but he seemed to draw it out of her. ''Redheads have taken a lot of bad press.''

''So have men who race cars for a living.'' Rick gave her a pointed stare. ''Any stereotype is a distortion.''

''Maybe you're right.'' Tracey looked at him curiously. Was he for real?

''Tracey!'' James Danvers exclaimed as he walked toward her. ''The press wants pictures of you with your crew.''

Tracey immediately turned around to flash a brilliant smile at her father. ''I was just . . . making Mr. Masters' acquaintance," she said in an unnaturally high voice.

"A pleasure, sir." Rick extended his hand to James.

"Sorry that we never had the opportunity to race against each other," James said as he shook hands.

"I'm not. I doubt if I would have stood a chance," Rick's voice held a note of admiration.

"You'll have the chance to race against my daughter. She's driving in the rally next week and then the upcoming Daytona 500."

"So I've heard," Rick replied automatically. He was still trying to steady his breathing. What was the matter with him? He had almost wanted to kiss Tracey Danvers right in the middle of the exhibition tent.

"I've had enough of hosing down those dirty cars," Troy pronounced as he approached, a sponge in his hands. "I don't care how much money we make for charity."

"All for a good cause, Troy," Tracey reminded him sweetly.

"I don't see you out there," Troy pointed out.

"Rick, what do you mean by sending some kid to me for Daytona passes?" Skid grumbled, ignoring the rest of the group that had gathered around Tracey's car. "Listen, we can't go around giving out free—" He broke off mid-sentence as he suddenly noticed Tracey. "You're the girl from the track," he blurted out.

An awkward silence descended.

"Let me do the honors," Rick volunteered smoothly. "Skid, this is Tracey Danvers. You know her brother, Troy. And, of course, you recognize their father—James Danvers.''

Tracey felt Troy and her father turn surprised looks in her direction. "I forgot. Rick and his crew chief and I met the other day—it must've slipped my mind."

"What?" Troy demanded.

Tracey flashed him a silencing look. "It didn't seem like a big deal."

"Interesting," Skid commented as his eyes moved back and forth between Tracey and Troy, resting finally on Tracey.

"And what exactly interests you about us, Mr. Parker?" Tracey asked.

His pebble-colored eyes narrowed slightly. "Maybe because you're twins you'll have a special advantage over the rest of the drivers."

"Skid," Rick began. "There's nothing—"

"There's no advantage," Tracey cut in, stressing the last word heavily, "except quick thinking and good driving."

Skid smiled, showing his small, sharp teeth. "I don't know. Mind reading could help tremendously when you're driving and Troy is in the pit. It might even relieve you of some of the stress of being alone in a car going almost two hundred miles an hour. He could also give you a sense of where all the other drivers are on the field."

"We don't 'mind read' as you call it. That's for psychics. We just have a feeling or a sense of the other's emotions." Tracey knew he was baiting her and she was trying to hold her temper back.

Troy nodded vigorously. "That's right. It's more like emotion than thought."

Rick's eyes flickered over Tracey. "Troy can sense *all* of your emotions?"

Tracey stifled a laugh into a semblance of a cough. Rick was obviously referring to the sudden connection they'd felt for each other. "Not all of them—no."

"I understand you intend to qualify for the Daytona 500, Miss Danvers?" Skid asked.

"I do and I will," Tracey pronounced. "The rally is just the beginning. I intend to race in NASCAR events."

"I see." Skid studied her for a few minutes. "No house, white picket fence, and kids for you, huh?"

The thought froze in her brain. "I want those things, too—in time." She tried to keep her voice cool. To her surprise, a picture of a small boy with Rick's black hair and grey eyes popped into her head—a boy about Danny's age. Was she crazy? She hardly knew Rick Masters.

"Rick, what do you think Miss Danvers' chances of winning are?" Skid asked slyly.

He hesitated, measuring his response for a moment. "I can't answer that," he began slowly. What was the matter with Skid asking a question like that? "Anymore than I can say if I'll win. None of us can tell until we're behind that wheel with forty other drivers breathing down our necks. Who knows? It's partly the driver and partly the car."

"Speaking of that—I'm interested in that new engine of yours, Rick," James Danvers cut in. "since I've been working with engineers on a new one of my own. Will it be ready for Daytona?''

''I'm not sure,'' Rick revealed. ''It's got some problems in the cooling system. I don't know if I want to risk it just yet.''

''We're working on the problem, though,'' Skid added smoothly. ''It'll be ready for the Daytona 500.''

Rick rolled his eyes at his crew chief. ''We *hope* it'll be ready.''

''It's your design, right?'' Troy asked.

Rick nodded. He sensed Skid was trying to figure out how much competition Tracey was going to be, and he didn't like his crew chief's tactics. Rick had tried to change the conversation a couple times, but with his usual brashness, Skid didn't seem to notice. But then Rick himself was having difficulty trying to follow the conversation, since his eyes kept straying back to Tracey. He liked the way her skin glowed with a touch of honey from the sun, bringing out the gold strands in her red hair.

Then Rick was drawn out of his reverie by Troy's question: ''Why did you get out of racing, Rick, and start designing engines?''

Tracey saw Rick's body stiffen and she could've kicked Troy for being so inquisitive.

''It's hard to say . . . a lot of things came together at once and the time seemed right to try something besides racing.'' Rick heard the sound in his mind of his car slamming against the wall. Each part of the crash was like a slow motion frame of a film he had memorized.

"Maybe I'm crazy to start it all up again, but it was something I had to do."

"I think we all have to be a little crazy to want to drive a car almost two hundred miles per hour lap after lap," Tracey said. She knew Rick wasn't telling them everything, that he was thinking of the accident, and maybe something more.

"Crazy. And always on the edge of losing control. There's nothing like it." Rick grinned with one corner of his mouth, his eyes back on Tracey. His emotions were beginning to feel a little out of control. Why couldn't he stop thinking about her? He had to keep his mind on why he had come to Daytona in the first place. He had to keep his mind on the upcoming race.

"I agree." Tracey's thoughts raced like an engine. Did she want to start a friendship with a man whose only place in her life was that of a competitor? Even worse, could she help herself from doing so?

Chapter Three

Tracey looked up, trying not to squint in the hot Florida sun. It was only ten o'clock in the morning and yet the temperature had already climbed into the upper eighties. They'd had one cold spell back in December, but now the temperature was almost as hot as mid-summer. The heat was made even more intense by the padded and insulated racing suit she was wearing. She wore the protective suit even for practice runs, because one of the first things her father had instilled in her was the need for safety at all times. But it could be excruciatingly uncomfortable at times.

She held her hand up across her forehead to screen out the glare of the sun as she searched for Troy on the track at the International Raceway. She smiled. He was on the opposite straightaway, finishing his tenth lap, and the silver Thunderbird was finally performing like a dream.

The car roared past her as she watched Troy take his final lap. His driving was good; he took every turn with precision, never straying too close to the outside walls that circled the track. Troy could make it as a driver himself if he wanted to, she thought for the hundredth time.

As she watched the silver streak moving across the opposite side of the track, she felt the excitement of the rally growing closer.

But the rally reminded her of Rick Masters—the man she was destined to race against.

Her face flushed with remembrance of those moments in the tent when she and Rick had been unable to tear their eyes away from each other.

Tracey hadn't been prepared for the stir of excitement Rick had brought into her life. She thought she was immune to those feelings after discovering she was only necessary to Roger as a stepping-stone in his career. But that was three years ago. She was older and wiser now. Determined not to get hurt again, she had spent the last few years single-mindedly pursuing her goal of becoming a stock car driver.

But somehow that all changed since Rick appeared on the scene.

Tracey had been so preoccupied with the image of Rick Masters the last few days that, more than once, Troy had to ask a question two or three times to get an answer. She'd sternly told herself that she *must* get Rick out of her thoughts, but somehow those grey eyes kept showing up. Could she trust him? Was he the tough driver she'd overheard in the garage, or the smiling man who charmed a young boy with his autograph?

She gave a groan and brushed the damp tendrils of hair off the back of her neck. She couldn't afford to have her stomach in knots over Rick. Too many people were counting on her. *I've just got to get him out of my mind. This type of obsession could interfere with the upcoming rally.*

With a start, Tracey realized that Troy had brought the Thunderbird to a halt in front of her.

He jumped out of the car and then whipped off his helmet. His brown hair waved boyishly on his forehead. "Do you believe that run? Your car is running incredibly fast. Did you catch my time on that last lap?"

"What? Oh yes. . . . " She shook her head slightly to clear her mind, and looked down at the stopwatch in her hand. She had to at least try to pay attention to what was going on. "Great! Over one-eighty. Did the engine seem to choke at all?"

"No problem. Everything ran smooth as glass."

She gave up a prayer of silent thanks. She didn't think she could work on that engine one more day.

"Tracey, what's wrong with you?"

She tried to avoid his glance. Her twin would detect a lie in a moment if he could see her face. "I guess I'm just a little jittery before the rally. I want us to do well. I want us to win."

He nodded in understanding. "Why don't you take it for a spin? That should reassure you."

She took his helmet and walked around to the driver's side of the car. As she slipped in through the window onto the padded seat, she felt the usual excitement that always descended over her. Being behind the wheel was one of the most exhilarating feelings she could imagine. Except being in Rick Masters' arms—

no, she stopped herself. She wouldn't let him continue to haunt her thoughts here on the track.

Before she had a chance to start the engine, a man slid onto the seat beside her. Normally, only one seat was in a NASCAR Thunderbird, with every instrument positioned for the driver's convenience, but an extra one had been added for the practise runs. Assuming it was Troy, Tracey strapped her safety harness on and pressed the ignition button to start the engine.

"Troy, why are you—" she broke off suddenly as she turned her head and realized her passenger was none other than Rick Masters himself.

"Rick!" she exclaimed in surprise. "What are you doing here?"

Her reaction seemed to amuse him. "I'm going to ride in your car as you drive around the track," he patiently explained. "You were wondering if you 'measure up.' I found myself wondering the same thing."

She turned her face forward, looking through the windshield. How could she concentrate with a world-famous driver like Rick next to her? She was just a rookie. "I don't think it's such a good idea." Her eyes darted back to him. *Oh God! Why did he look so handsome in his white polo shirt and khaki trousers?* His black hair appeared to have almost a blue sheen against the starkly white material.

"Why not?" Rick asked reasonably. "You drive. I sit. Seems simple enough."

"This situation is far from simple."

"Because you lied the other day at the track?"

"I didn't lie," she protested. "If you'd asked, I would've told you I was James Danvers' daughter."

Rick eyed her skeptically. "I think you liked having me at a disadvantage. But am I that much of a threat?"

She shrugged with pretended indifference. "You're just another driver to me."

"And you haven't missed me in the last few days?"

She was clutching the steering wheel tightly, her breathing slightly erratic. How could he know how much he had haunted her thoughts the last few days?

"Come on, Tracey, the engine's running." He handed over her helmet, his smile warm and sincere. "Let's take it for a spin."

She took the helmet and jammed it resolutely on her head. She could do it. It's what she'd trained her whole life for.

As she pressed her foot down on the pedal, the car shot out quickly into the middle of the track. Rick placed his own helmet on, and with one brief glance at Tracey's set face, he fastened his eyes intently on the track in front of them.

She increased the pressure on the pedal and then shifted gears rapidly and smoothly. The speed went up to a hundred miles per hour within the first ten seconds. She felt the usual thrill of the power of the engine under her as she pressed the pedal down even further. The speedometer inched up past one-hundred-and-fifty miles per hour. The wheel responded to her slightest touch and the car held the track as if it were almost glued to it. At the first curve, she shifted down to a lower gear and took it high on the embankment, but with a safe enough distance from the wall. Once she reached the straightaway again, she increased the speed almost to one-hundred-and-eighty miles per hour.

She flashed a quick look at her passenger to see if she had impressed him, but his face was immobile, hard and set as he concentrated on the track in front of him.

Tracey dismissed him from her mind quickly, though, as she immediately turned her concentration back to the track. She knew that even a momentary distraction could cause an accident.

As she took the second curve, which was even sharper than the first one, again dropping the speed, she steered through it somewhat in the middle of the track. The last thing she wanted to do was to take foolhardy risks that would make her seem like a juvenile driver.

''The car seems to respond well,'' Rick shouted over the roar of the engine.

As soon as she completed the second curve, she increased the speed again and skillfully maneuvered the car down the track. When they reached the pit area, she started to slow down and then halted in front of Troy.

Tracey clicked the engine off and removed her helmet, shaking her silky hair free. Although she tried to be nonchalant about her actions, inside she was disappointed that Rick hadn't made any comment about her driving. She knew she was good and he must know it now, too.

Rick took off his own helmet, his glance inexorably

drawn to her tousled hair. "Not bad. Thanks for the ride, Tracey."

"That's it?" Tracey asked. She wanted more than that.

"You want a critique? Okay." Rick paused. "How about over dinner tonight?"

Tracey felt a flicker of delight inside. "Are you asking me for a date?"

"Why not? We seem to have a lot in common—with racing and everything." Rick tried to keep the invitation nonchalant. In fact, he was totally captivated by her—he had wanted to pick up the phone a hundred times over the last few days. But every time he did, it seemed Skid had a new emergency with the stock car. But this morning he'd overheard Jake say Tracey would be at the Raceway, so Rick sneaked out before Skid could catch him again. "And I could tell you what I think about your driving."

She laughed to cover her annoyance. "What an invitation! How could a woman refuse? But—"

"Great, that's settled then. I'll pick you up at eight."

"But . . . as I was saying . . . this woman will refuse," she added with feigned sweetness.

He simply continued on: "We could go anywhere you like. Do you prefer seafood? The Trackside has excellent swordfish—and there's a dance floor."

"Didn't you hear me? I just refused to go out with you!"

He still seemed unmoved. "Or we could try an Italian place I know. Their linguine is the best I've had anywhere. Even in Italy."

Tracey ran her tongue over dry lips. She had to continue before her convictions dissolved. "No seafood. No Italian. No dinner. If we need to talk, we can talk here."

Rick backed off. She was gun-shy of relationships. He couldn't press her too hard. But more than anything, he wanted to be with her tonight. Maybe that was foolish—after all, she was his competition. But he suddenly couldn't care less. That reckless streak of his youth he thought was gone was being resurrected by the charms of Tracey Danvers.

She plunged on before she lost her resolve. "Look, it's best if we don't start something here that could—" She paused to catch her breath. "That could . . . have an effect on our racing against each other."

A shadow of annoyance briefly passed over Rick's face. "I never let anything interfere with my edge as a driver. Competitive racing is just that—a business. But maybe you can't handle—"

"I can handle anything," she cut him off.

Rick said nothing, but the significant lifting of his brows spoke volumes.

Tracey made a small fist and shook it threateningly. "Now look here, buster—"

"Wait a minute, settle down." He caught her hand in his own larger one. "Turnabout's fair play?"

A reluctant smile spread over Tracey's face, showing a tiny dimple in her right cheek. "For the trick I played on you at the raceway?"

He nodded with a boyish smile. "You have to admit you should take a little ribbing back."

"Are we back to games again or are you going to tell me what you really think about my driving?"

"The games are over. But no date, no advice." Rick continued in a light voice. He was determined to break down her distrust of him. "And I do want to see you."

And I want to see you, Tracey echoed inside. But it wouldn't be smart. Competitors. That's what they were—no, it was worse than that—he was her *chief* competition, as her father had pointed out. And yet . . . when Rick smiled at her with those warm grey eyes, she was lost to all reason.

As though aware of the conflicting feeling inside of her, Rick further prompted: "Well? Is it dinner tonight or not?" He looked down, turning her hand over in his, trying not to let her see the eagerness in his face.

She couldn't deny the spark of excitement at the prospect. But her whole future was hanging in the balance.

"No," Tracey said finally with a firm voice. She took on a regretful undertone as she went on: "Talking here is one thing. We're both racers, we need to exchange ideas, and I could use your advice. But, let's be realistic. We'll need an edge to race against each other and that will be gone if we . . . ," her voice trailed off.

Rick let her hand fall reluctantly. She was probably right. That recklessness had gotten him into trouble before. "Maybe you're right at that. It probably wouldn't work out." He gave her a half-hearted smile and quickly slid out of the car.

Tracey slowly lifted herself out of the car and

watched his retreating figure. Why did she feel so let down? Wasn't that what she really wanted? She saw him stop, say a few words to Troy and then drive off in his vintage Chevrolet. A tumble of confused thoughts and feelings assailed her, but her pride concealed her inner turmoil when Troy approached her.

"You looked great out there. I know Rick was impressed."

She felt her face flush slightly, and hoped that Troy would think it was the heat. "I guess so. He didn't say much."

"Really?" he seemed genuinely taken aback. "He told me just now before he left that he thought you drove like a real pro."

"Did he?" she exclaimed in surprise and delight.

Troy nodded as he started to collect his racing gear.

"But he didn't tell me . . . ," she trailed off in puzzlement. What did he really think? Was he holding back to try to get her to go out with him? The thought of her meaning that much to him that he would try subterfuge to get a date with her, delighted her even more. One thing she did know: She couldn't help the tiny glow those words lit inside of her. Tracey had to admit to herself that there was something undeniable between them—something she just couldn't ignore. If he accepted her as a driver, an equal, maybe she could start to trust him a little.

"You know. . . . " An idea suddenly occurred to Tracey. "I think . . . uh . . . we should go somewhere tonight and relax a little before the rally starts next week. I don't have a date tonight, do you?"

"Free as a bird."

"Let's go have a few drinks and maybe dinner."

"Great idea. Any suggestions?"

She pretended to think for a few moments. "Perhaps somewhere with good seafood like . . . The Trackside?"

Troy looked at her in mild surprise. "Okay with me, but I thought you didn't like places that fancy."

She gave an artless little gesture with her hands. "Sometimes it's good for a change of pace, and I like dressing up at times, you know."

"No!" he mocked. "I never see you out of those grubby overalls."

She made a face at him. "All the more reason for it."

He grinned. "Okay. Let's get cleaned up and have dinner about seven-thirty."

As he walked off whistling, Tracey was ashamed at having taken advantage of her twin's trusting nature. That was the first time she had deliberately deceived him. And all for a man whom she couldn't even decide whether she could trust or not. She almost laughed to herself at the absurdity of her own behavior. Would Rick even be there tonight and, if he were, what would he think about her trying to follow up on a date she had just turned down? It was no use going back now, she told herself resolutely. She had decided to make the next move and he could make of it what he chose.

When Tracey and Troy walked into The Trackside's lounge a few hours later, the room seemed to be throbbing with rock music and overly loud conversation. It was a popular spot in Daytona for the racing crowd and one of the few that was not generally filled with tourists.

"What do you think? A drink?" Troy asked.

Tracey nodded as she started to weave her way through the crowd, looking for an empty table.

"It's really packed tonight," Troy observed as he looked around. The room was dim but he was able to spot a few friends and wave to them. The music was so loud, though, he knew it was pointless to try to even shout to them. "Lots of people here who are going to be in the rally."

Tracey's gaze followed Troy's, her eyes sweeping the room for one particular person. "You're right. I guess I wasn't the only one with the idea of coming here tonight to blow off a little steam. I see at least three other drivers we know."

The waitress who was wearing an extremely short black skirt and very high heels came over to their table. "What will you have?" Her eyes were fixed on Troy's handsome features.

He smiled, blithely unaware of his impact on the girl. "I'll have a rum punch."

She flashed him a flirtatious smile and was about to turn away, when Tracey stopped her. "Miss?"

The waitress heaved a loud sigh. "Yes?" She reluctantly poised her pen above the order form.

"I'd like a wine spritzer, please."

"Right. Sorry," she said in an unapologetic tone.

When she left, Tracey turned to Troy with some amusement. "I think you've already scored a hit here."

"What?" He was still trying to spot racers he knew.

"The waitress. Or didn't you notice anything?"

"Huh? Oh, yeah, but I've got more important things on my mind." He motioned slightly to the left with his head. "Do you see who's over in the corner?"

Tracey tried to look sideways without turning her head, but she couldn't really see whom Troy was looking at. "I can't see who it is without turning and staring, and embarrassing both of us."

He lowered his voice slightly as though about to reveal a startling secret. "It's Paco Carrera."

"What!" she couldn't help exclaiming.

Troy nodded sagely.

"What's he doing here? You don't think he's actually going to run in the rally? Not after his last accident in Atlanta!"

"I don't know." There was a thoughtful look in his eyes. "Unless—"

"Unless what? Come on!"

He leaned forward conspiratorially. "Well, you know Carrera was the winner at Darlington two years in a row; then, six months ago, the race came down to a contest between Rick Masters and him. They were neck and neck right up till the end, when Rick pulled out ahead of him and won the race. After that defeat, Carrera's had nothing but a series of crashes and bad luck. His car didn't even finish in the top ten for any race during the last six months. Rumor is he went back to Miami to lick his wounds and find new sponsorship.''

She digested this information, following where Troy's train of thought was going. ''So you think he's here to drive in the rally and try to get his reputation back?''

''And maybe take revenge on Rick. Apparently, he blames Rick for his run of bad luck.''

''That's superstitious rubbish,'' Tracey scoffed.

Troy shrugged. ''You know how racers are.''

''Why the rally? It's mainly publicity.''

''Why not?'' Troy countered. ''He could start at the rally. Beat Rick, and then get enough publicity to attract sponsorship for the Daytona 500. Or at least a contract to race for someone.''

The waitress came back with their drinks, serving Troy's with an extra flourish. When she didn't get a response from Troy, she then set Tracey's drink down sharply in front of her, causing some of the contents to spill on the table.

''I'm going to have to stop coming here with you, Troy, if I value my life,'' Tracey observed as she watched the waitress saunter off.

Grinning, Troy leaned back in his chair. ''This looks like it's going to be one interesting rally.''

She couldn't help wondering if Rick was aware of Paco's presence in Daytona, and how he was going to handle his fellow driver's fiercely competitive spirit. ''I can't believe Carrera would do anything stupid—the last thing anybody needs is a rogue driver. There's

no reason for him to take the defeat as anything else
but—''

''Look who else just came in!'' Troy interrupted in
an excited voice. ''Rick Masters. I guess he'll find out
about his competitor fairly soon.''

Tracey couldn't help the warm glow that flowed
through her. Somehow she felt Rick's presence before
she even saw him. As she turned her head slightly, she
saw his unmistakable jet-black hair and deeply tanned
face. He was taller than most of the other men in the
room, and he radiated a quiet strength that drew her
like a magnet. She felt the heat rise to her face, and
took a sip of her drink to cool herself down.

''Perhaps we should invite him to join us,'' she
suggested innocently to her twin as she placed her glass
back on the table.

He looked at her incredulously. ''Are you kidding?
I thought you were angry with him?''

She forced a demure smile. ''Maybe I was a little
too hasty. Since he's going to be in the rally, we might
as well be friendly.''

Troy looked bemused at this sudden change in his
sister. He started to wave at Rick and slowly a smile
spread over his face. ''Maybe asking him over would
be a good idea at that. You should see the bombshell
he's got on his arm.''

Tracey couldn't help turning her head to look and,
suddenly, all the pleasure of the evening left her. The
woman Rick was with was obviously his date for the
evening. She was a petite blond, with an attractive
figure revealed in a softly draped pink silk dress. And

she seemed to be looking at Rick with a particularly repellent look of adoration.

Tracey was filled with disappointment and then she was angry with herself for feeling that way. She had no hold on Rick; they weren't even seeing each other. So why did the sight of Rick with another woman bother her? Maybe because he had asked *her* out this evening first. It was more than a little irritating to know he had so quickly replaced her with another woman.

"Oh, good, he spotted us," Troy said as he motioned them over, much to Tracey's chagrin.

As Rick strolled over, Tracey noted the blond stayed where she was, though she kept her eyes on Rick the whole time.

All of the sudden, the music seemed like it was throbbing in an excessively loud manner and Tracey's temples started to pound.

"Surprising to see you two here." Rick emphasized the last word, with a long look at Tracey.

"Troy felt we should have a night off for a change," Tracey rushed to explain before her twin had a chance to open his mouth.

"Good idea," Rick agreed. "The important thing is that you're here." He didn't care why she changed her mind, he thought as his eyes skimmed over her slim figure encased in her chartreuse jumpsuit. Unlike her racing suit, this one clung to her slim curves and contrasted with her vivid, flame-colored hair.

Tracey's brows shot up in puzzlement. Rick seemed genuinely glad to see her, yet he had brought another woman instead.

Troy started to signal the waitress. "Do you want to join us, Rick?"

"Oh, Troy, I see the maitre d' motioning to us. I think our table is ready," Tracey broke in, wanting to get away from Rick's penetrating grey eyes as soon as possible. She didn't know how to hide the stab of jealousy that had overcome her at the sight of the blond.

Troy's face fell with disappointment, but Tracey pretended not to see it.

She rose quickly and pulled her brother up with her. "Sorry, perhaps next time."

As she attempted to breeze past Rick, though, she heard him whisper, "Coward!" for her ears alone. She just set her chin in a stubborn line and walked away, giving no indication of having heard him.

As they reached the ornately decorated, black and gold dining room, it seemed almost too quiet after the noise they had left behind. Once seated, Troy turned to his twin with an unusually terse expression. "What's the matter with you, Tracey? You wanted him to come over for a drink and, once he did, you jumped at the chance to get away from him."

"I didn't want to miss our table," Tracey explained lamely as she tried to suppress her chaotic feelings. Her emotions were doing a seesaw every time she saw Rick—he must think her a complete fool. "You know how difficult they can be here. They'll give your table away in minutes if you don't come when they call you."

He regarded her quizzically for a moment. "The

least you could've done is invite him to join us for dinner.''

"Let's just drop it. Okay, Troy?'' she responded shortly. She had to get herself under control again.

He shook his head, apparently baffled by this side of his sister he had never seen before.

Once seated, Tracey turned to him with an appeasing look. "Let's not argue, Troy. The last thing we need is to be at each other before a big race.''

He slowly broke into a rueful grin. "Okay. I guess we both have pre-rally jitters.''

Tracey let out a long, audible breath. Being at odds with Troy was not how she wanted to spend the evening. It was difficult enough to accept how events had turned out. Her thoughts involuntarily went back to the blond, and she wondered what her relationship was to Rick. Tracey knew about the adoring followers who chased drivers around from track to track, but she had hoped Rick didn't go in for that sort of thing.

"Do you want to order?'' Troy broke into her reflections as the waiter approached.

Tracey pushed the unwelcome thoughts to the back of her mind and determinedly tried to study the menu. It was no use spoiling their entire evening simply because she couldn't sort out her emotions. "I'd like the special: grilled swordfish.''

"I'll have the same. What about wine?''

"I think I'll pass and just finish this drink.'' She motioned at her spritzer.

Troy nodded in agreement. "It's not good to drink too much before an upcoming race anyway.''

After giving their order to the tuxedo-clad waiter, they sat back to watch the floor show. The singer was a woman with dark hair who had a haunting voice. She sang some popular tunes that Tracey recognized, and then she broke into a melancholy love song. The notes seemed to penetrate to the very core of Tracey's being, as she was swept away by the most timeless of themes—true love.

The singer's voice broke slightly with emotion as she reached the end of the song, and Tracey felt her eyes fill with tears. She flicked her eyes in irritation. What was the matter with her? Why was she getting all teary-eyed about Rick being with another woman? She'd only met him twice. It wasn't as if they even knew each other all that well.

She couldn't let this attraction to him get out of hand. When she was around him, she acted too rash, too impetuous. And she couldn't afford to give free reign to those aspects of her personality. She had done that before, and it brought her only heartache. Besides, too much was riding on her being focused and committed to her racing career.

As the song ended, Tracey took a deep breath and let it out slowly. She reminded herself that racing was her life and there was no room for Rick Masters. Nothing would stand in the way of her achieving her dream of winning.

Chapter Four

Tracey forced a smile on her face—a brave front, but it was the best she could do under the circumstances.

By the time their dinner was served, she had control of herself again and was chatting amicably with Troy. They ate their swordfish with zestful appreciation, topping it off with generous slices of frozen key lime pie and steaming cups of coffee.

"That was absolutely delicious, Troy. We need to do this more often."

"Are you kidding?" Troy exclaimed in exaggerated horror. "Your car is balanced for your weight. A few extra pounds and you could throw the whole race."

She laughed in delight at the ridiculousness of Troy's response, yet she realized he was also right. Although she burned a lot of calories in nervous energy, she still had to monitor her diet. The cars were delicately balanced for each driver's weight, so she couldn't afford to deviate much more than a few pounds.

As they were finishing their coffee, Troy suddenly said in a low undertone: "Don't look up, Tracey, but Paco Carrera is coming over to our table."

"What?" She didn't have time to say anything else,

because Paco was already slapping Troy on the back good-naturedly.

"Danvers, right? You remember me, of course?" he asked in supreme self-confidence.

"Mr. Carrera." Troy acknowledged with a polite nod. "We met last year at the Darlington race. I don't think you've met my sister, Tracey."

Tracey smiled and held her hand out. Instead of shaking her hand, he leaned over and kissed it in continental fashion. She tried not to smile at his studied romantic air, although she couldn't deny the attractiveness of his dark, Latin looks. In fact, his coloring was similar to Rick's but his shoulders weren't as broad and his stature was somewhat shorter. His dress was also considerably more dramatic. He wore a splashy tropical shirt and raw silk pants in a bright shade of turquoise.

"Tell me it's not true—the rumor I heard. That this beautiful woman intends to drive in the rally." He directed his question at Troy. "I ask myself—why?"

"Because I happen to like it, Mr. Carrera," Tracey responded spiritedly. "And it's true—Troy and I are going to be in the rally."

"I see." He nodded gravely. "Don't get me wrong—I think it's great that women are finally getting into racing. In fact, I can't believe it's taken this long."

Tracey knew he was lying and, surprisingly, she didn't feel angry; she was amused. "I believe it, considering the difficulties I know other woman racers have had."

Paco gave Tracey a smile that showed off his startlingly perfect teeth. He probably had them all capped, she mused wryly.

"Actually, I came over to see if you'd like to dance, Miss Danvers."

Tracey noted that the singer and her back-up musicians had started playing soft, romantic dance music; the lights had dimmed, and a few couples were indeed drifting toward the small dance floor. Troy's eyes were bright with expectation, and she could hardly disappoint him.

She held her hand out to Paco. "I'd love to."

Then she stood up and waited for his reaction. For a moment, he seemed comically dismayed at Tracey's height, since she was on eye level with him. His poise was even more shaken when he looked down and saw Tracey was not wearing high heels. But his smile remained intact—if a little strained.

They walked to the center of the dance floor and started to move to the soft beat of the music. Paco held Tracey a shade too closely, but he seemed to be scrutinizing her in an impersonal, assessing manner. He's probably trying to figure out how much competition I'm going to be to him, Tracey speculated. At least he didn't try to hide it.

"Is it true that you're also driving in the Florida pace car rally, Mr. Carrera?" Tracey asked. She might as well make conversation since she was trapped for at least one dance, and she *was* curious.

He smiled again—that flash of dazzling white against the olive skin. "I am, and looking forward to it. But please call me Paco."

"Okay, *Paco,* but I'm surprised that you'd be interested in a little rally like ours."

"Not so little. It's still a national event and there's a lot of publicity connected with it," he responded somewhat defensively. "That never hurts when looking for sponsorship."

"The bane of modern racing," Tracey replied in a light tone. "We can never get away from it."

Paco's head dropped in resignation, his own sponsorship problems obviously on his mind. "In your father's day, it was easier, but today it's so expensive to race, we can't get by without the sponsorship. What about you?"

Tracey deliberately gave him a bland look. "What about me?"

"I mean, how are you being sponsored?"

"My father has arranged for all of that," she answered evasively. She actually knew about every item and clause of their sponsor contract, but she had no intention of revealing that information to Paco, however charming he appeared.

Fortunately, he accepted this answer. "But what a subject to discuss when I'm holding a lovely woman in my arms."

She managed a small smile at the compliment, and had to concede that she was delighted to change the subject. "What would you like to discuss?" she asked, her green eyes sparkling. It was easy to join in with the mood of light-hearted conversation. After the emotionally-charged exchanges she had had with Rick Masters, it seemed a pleasant interlude. With Paco, her heart wasn't in danger.

Paco's arms tightened imperceptibly. This was a game he obviously felt he was an expert at; he knew all the right moves. "We could talk about how beautiful it would be to take a moonlit stroll down the beach, so I could watch your hair blow gently in the breeze," he offered with a gleam in his dark eyes.

In spite of herself, Tracey chuckled. This man really knew how to lay on the flattery, however insincere the source.

"You two seem to be having a good time," a familiar voice broke in. Tracey didn't even have to turn around to know it was Rick Masters. What was he still doing here? Since she hadn't seen him in the dining room, she thought by this time he would have left with the blond.

Paco's eyes grew guarded, but he said nothing.

"Mind if I cut in?" Rick asked.

Before Paco could answer, Rick snapped up Tracey's hand and, with a quick motion, pulled her into his arms and continued the dance that Paco had started.

"What do you think you're doing?" she demanded indignantly, straining against his arms. Paco was still standing where they had left him. He now looked openly dismayed.

"That should be obvious. I'm dancing with you."

"That was unbelievably rude . . . to just leave poor Paco standing there." Her voice rose an octave.

"He's already dancing with someone else," Rick inclined his head toward a dark-haired woman now in

Paco's arms. Actually, Rick felt a stab of conscience, but the darker emotion he'd felt when seeing Tracey dance with Paco was stronger. Seeing her in Paco's arms had made Rick want to knock him down—that scared him. He'd never felt that type of jealousy before. "Besides, I could tell you wanted me to cut in."

"I wouldn't count on that."

He pulled her close, seemingly oblivious to her retort. "Do you know what I really thought?"

"What?"

"I thought—'she walks in beauty, like the night.' "

Tracey pulled back, startled. *"You're* quoting poetry?"

Rick gave her a wounded look. "What's so unusual about that? I happen to like poetry. And having a mother who was an English teacher doesn't hurt."

"Somehow, it just doesn't fit with . . . ," she trailed off, not quite sure of what she wanted to say.

"The image of a speed jockey?" Rick offered. "I told you there's more to me than meets the eye."

Unlike dancing with Paco, the pressure of Rick's chest against hers was affecting her senses, and her thoughts were coming in a tumbled mess. Why did he always have this effect on her?

"And don't worry, I'm not angry with you for changing your mind and deciding to meet me here after all," he went on in a friendly tone.

"What do you mean? I never agreed to meet you here. This just happens to be the place where Troy and I decided to have dinner." It sounded unconvincing even to her.

His eyes gleamed in amused disbelief. She couldn't be totally immune to him if she showed up here this evening. At least he hoped so, or he was making a big fool of himself.

"Anyway, you certainly didn't lose any time in finding a replacement for the evening," Tracey rebuked him with a toss of her red hair.

"What are you talking about?" he asked in genuine surprise.

"Oh, come on!" she retorted, irked by his pretended innocence. "The blond I saw you with earlier . . . your date for the evening."

The blank look in his eyes was slowly replaced by a sharpened awareness. "Were you jealous?"

She looked down to avoid those penetrating eyes. "Of course not. I don't care what you do, or who you do it with. It doesn't make any difference to me."

"You don't need to be jealous. She's not a girlfriend. She's a reporter doing a story on the rally drivers."

Tracey felt the dark cloud melt away, but she tried not to show it.

"Satisfied?" he asked softly.

"You have to admit that my conclusions weren't unreasonable."

"There's a lot you don't know about me. What do you say, Tracey? Get to know me. We know we have one thing in common."

"Racing?"

"No, Paco. He wants to beat both of us."

As their eyes met, Tracey's mouth twitched with amusement. Her shoulders started to shake, and then she couldn't control her burst of laughter. Laughing, too, Rick spun her around the dance floor.

"Rick, you're awful," Tracey finally managed to get out. "And in our profession, I have to be careful about the people I socialize with."

Rick smiled down at her, his eyes almost tender. "The track is one thing. This is a different type of race."

She looked into his boldly handsome face. "It's still all a game to you Rick."

"And if it isn't?" His eyes seemed to be questioning her.

"I'm serious about what I'm doing. Racing is my whole life, and you—"

"Race against you? Is that it?" His face hardened slightly. "I take competition seriously, make no mistake about that."

"No one could want to win more than me."

"Except maybe me."

Tracey's mouth thinned slightly. "Good. Then we both know where we stand. Two people in pursuit of the same goal, and only one can win."

He leaned down and kissed her lightly on the lips before she had time to react. "There are different ways of winning."

She pulled away from him, anxious to escape his disturbing presence. "I think the music is ending."

Rick watched her rejoin her brother. Darn it! What had made him kiss her like that on the dance floor? He was losing it. He had to try to go slowly. She was starting her career and she was unsure of herself. Besides, she did have a point. They were competitors. They would race against each other. But the very feel of her skin tonight had sent all rational thought out of his mind. He had to see her again.

Watch it, he warned himself, this was one race he might not win.

Tracey awoke the next morning with a sense of something vaguely being wrong. She slowly stretched her arms above her head and flexed her toes while she tried to detect what had triggered this feeling. She leaned up on her elbows and looked around her bedroom with its pine floors and light oak furniture. Everything seemed to be in its place. She dropped back down on the pillow and pulled her peach and green striped comforter up under her arms.

She strained her ears to hear any strange noises. She didn't hear anything. But that in itself was strange. There was always some type of noise going on. Troy and her father made enough noise stomping around the house for ten men.

The silence was odd and unnerving. She shook her head slightly in frustration; she just couldn't pinpoint anything. Then she glanced over at the small gilt clock next to her bed. It was eleven o'clock! She had slept the morning away.

She threw back the coverlet and jumped out of bed. It was too late to take a shower, and anyway she was just going to Jake's garage. She grabbed a pair of white shorts which had faded to a sandy beige and a bright red tee-shirt that had "Daytona 500" splashed across the front in large black letters. She ran a brush quickly through her hair and, at the last minute, put on a dash of cherry lipstick. She really didn't want to take time to do anymore; too much of the morning was already gone.

As Tracey quickly clattered down the stairs, she looked around in puzzlement. Where in the world was everyone? She walked into the kitchen and found it was empty like the rest of the house.

She inhaled the aroma of freshly brewed coffee. Someone had been up—and made a pot of coffee. She shrugged lightly and then helped herself to a cup. It was strong and black, just the way she liked it. As she slowly drank the coffee, she leaned against the counter and wondered whether the whole family had gone to Acapulco or Jake's.

When Tracey arrived at Jake's about half an hour later, she scanned the parking area but didn't see any of her family's cars. She walked around to the back entrance and heard two deep male voices: It was Jake's gravelly baritone talking to another man whose voice she couldn't make out. As she drew closer, she recognized who it was: Rick Masters. And he didn't sound too happy. Tracey's mind immediately went back to the dance they had shared the previous evening. Her face grew warm as she thought of how it felt to be held in his arms.

She was brought back to reality, however, when she heard Rick exclaim in some impatience: "What can I do about it?"

So Rick was having engine problems again! Tracey quietly crept closer to hear what they were saying.

"What about the Daytona 500?"

Jake didn't answer for a few moments. "If you get your people working with me round the clock, you *might* be ready. But this engine design is so experimental . . . ," he trailed off without finishing the rest of the sentence. They both knew that he would be lucky if the car were running.

"First the pace car blows a piston and I'm out of the rally—and now this," Rick emphasized the last word by slamming the palm of his hand against his car. He took a deep breath—there was no point in giving into his frustration. He had to find a way out. "It's been an eventful day, to say the least."

Tracey felt Rick's deep disappointment in the silence that followed. Missing the rally was one thing, but not being in one of the season's major races was another. She didn't want to see him miss that chance even if she were competing against him.

She entered the garage and saw Jake and Rick bent over the car engine. Rick immediately turned around as though he sensed her presence. Their eyes met, and it was as though they were still in that magic circle of the dance they shared last night. But she saw the troubled depths in his eyes and felt a tug of sympathy in her heart. Then he broke into the familiar daredevil smile that sent her pulses spinning. She had to stop herself from walking over to give him a hug of reassurance. Instead, she casually moved over to his car. "Engine trouble?" she inquired.

"Could be. Would you like to take a look for your-self?" he asked in an offhand, jesting way.

She colored slightly. "I think Jake's your man. If anybody can get your engine working, he can. With hard work and some luck...."

"It's surprising how fate can intervene with the best-laid plans," he replied enigmatically. Then he ducked back under the hood, seemingly occupied with his engine.

As she was still puzzling over his remark, Jake asked her quietly: "Did your father call you this morning?"

She shook her head, more baffled than ever.

Jake put an arm around her. "It was nothing real bad, but they had to take Troy to the hospital."

Fear quickened her heartbeat. "What happened?"

"Troy slipped on something . . . I don't know how. He hurt his ankle. I think it was badly sprained."

She sighed in relief. At least it wasn't a major accident. "I thought it was funny that no one was around the house this morning," she said almost to herself. "When did it happen?"

"About two hours ago."

"How's Troy feeling?"

Jake gave a short laugh. "He was more irritated than anything else. You know, at being out of commission for the rally."

Tracey's questioning eyes met Jake's calm gaze. He nodded and said: "I'm afraid so. He can't drive with a sprained ankle for at least a week or two and, as your team member, he has to drive."

How could this have happened? It was their first big

race and now Troy was injured. She closed her eyes, feeling silent and defeated. Then she thought about Troy and felt guilty and selfish. It was only a rally, after all. They would have the Daytona coming up soon. But still. . . .

"Look, let me drive you to the hospital, Tracey," Rick volunteered quietly. He was directly behind her.

"No thanks, I can drive myself." She had to fight the urge to lean back against his hard chest.

Rick slowly wiped the engine grease from his hands as he walked around in front of her. "I don't want you to drive alone, that's all."

She tried to read his face, but it seemed hidden. Maybe just this once she could lean on someone else. "All right—and thanks."

She got the name of the hospital from Jake, and then she gave him instructions in case her father called the garage looking for her.

In the meantime, Rick lowered the hood of his car with a loud slam. "It's up to you, Jake. I don't have more than a few weeks to get this car running. I'll send some of my guys over to work with you."

Jake smiled ruefully as he rubbed the back of his neck. "All I can do is try, and pray a lot."

Rick gave a short laugh and then escorted Tracey out to his restored white '57 Chevy. Once she was leaning back against the soft leather interior of his seats, she let out a tremulous sigh. She had been keyed up all morning, even more so since she had heard about Troy's accident. Much as she hated to admit it, Rick was probably right about her not driving. She needed a few minutes to gain back her equilibrium, although being in the car with him perhaps wasn't the best way to restore her peace of mind.

Driving along the coastal highway in silence, Rick glanced at Tracey's strained face. She had opened the window and the wind was blowing her red hair in a wild tangle. It surprised him to realize that he wanted nothing more than to smooth it down into its usual silky cascade and reassure her. He had never felt those protective feelings for a woman before—it was a new experience for him.

"It'll be okay, you know," he finally said.

Tracey turned her face from the window to give him a searching gaze. "I know. But why should you concern yourself? I mean with us, Troy and me. You could be working on your car or something."

He kept his eyes on the road. "I can't resist a damsel in distress."

She shot him a twisted smile. "I was hardly in 'distress.' All I needed was a ride to the hospital."

"Really?" He quirked his eyebrow questioningly. "How ungrateful of you. First I rescue you from Paco, that roving pseudo-Latin lecher, and then today I provide you with what I may call superior transport to the hospital when you're too emotionally overwrought to drive yourself."

Tracey chuckled softly as she pulled a wayward strand of hair away from her face. "This old Chevy?"

Rick looked as though she had mortally wounded him. "What? This is almost an antique. Every part has been replaced, the body has been restored—it runs perfectly. There's symmetry and beauty in every line.''

''You sound like a romantic, and that I don't believe.''

''Maybe you should believe it. I might be the poet of professional racing. I told you I liked poetry.''

She held up her hand in mock protest. ''Oh please—it's too ridiculous.'' However, she was intrigued.

His grey eyes shifted back to Tracey. ''You have to admit driving well *is* poetry.''

''Wait a minute—are you saying *my* driving is . . . poetry?'' she asked excitedly.

Rick hesitated. The warning bells were going off again. He wanted to be truthful with her—but he also knew she was still uncertain about herself as a driver. ''Yours is more like . . . blank verse.''

''What?'' Instantly she tensed.

''Rhythm and no rhyme.''

''Are you saying I don't drive well?'' she demanded.

Rick shook his head. He was treading water again, but she needed to hear the truth or she'd never be the driver she wanted to be. ''You're good—you pace well, with good control. But a driver has to match each part of the track with himself, like a rhyme. Textbook driving is one thing, but to be really good, you have to drive with your intuition.'' Rick's fingers spread out across the steering as his voice took on a persuasive quality.

Tracey felt as if the wind had been knocked out of her. Was he telling her what he really thought or was he trying to psyche her out before the race? He sounded sincere, but it was so difficult for her to let her guard down and trust him. "I'm not sure—"

"Let me show you."

She turned her face back toward the open window and replied shortly: "I don't need a teacher."

"Then I don't suppose you'd even consider driving in the Florida pace car rally with me," he asked casually.

Tracey was so startled by his suggestion that she couldn't respond for a few moments. Then she was glad that he couldn't see her face, or how her eyes involuntarily lit up excitedly in reaction to his statement. To be driving with him, a world-class driver whose very presence made her feel more fully alive than she had ever felt in her life, would be a situation she could have only dreamed of. But it could be a situation so frought with the danger of her own attraction to him, that she knew she couldn't agree. Besides, he was still the competition.

"Well?" he prompted.

"You know I can't drive in the rally with you."

"Why not?"

She made an impatient sound. "Because we're competitors. We race against each other, not *with* each other."

He smiled knowingly. "Face it, Tracey. You're afraid."

"Afraid of what?" she responded sarcastically. "I can hold my own with any other driver, including you."

Rick realized he was taking on trouble with Tracey

Danvers. But he couldn't resist. She reminded him of himself ten years ago—she was hungry to prove herself, and the proof was in the winning. "There's nothing wrong with accepting help when it's offered."

"Someone I could learn from, right?" Tracey bit her lip. She was a rookie and she could learn a lot from Rick. But it was more than that. She wanted to know him better—to be his friend.

Rick kept his eyes on the road, seemingly unaware of her conflicting emotions. "Maybe we both could learn something."

Tracey was surprised again by this unpredictable man. Did he really want to enter the rally with her, or was he trying to learn more about her as a competitor? If she lost the edge to win in racing, she knew her career was over before it even began. Yet her heart seemed to be telling her to trust him, to let herself go and believe in what was between them. But another part of her, the level-headed woman who had taken on a man's profession, just couldn't be sure.

"Sorry, Rick. I don't think you and I would make a good team."

"I don't know, we seemed to fit together pretty well last night at The Trackside."

Tracey cleared her throat as a sound of rebuke. "I meant as a driving team."

"You know, Tracey, maybe you chose the wrong profession. If you're afraid to take a risk, you'll never win any races. Risk-taking is the name of the game for us."

Her eyes fastened on his profile. The scar seemed

to stand out as a thin white streak against his dark cheek. "The kind of risk you're offering, I don't need." But part of her did. Part of her wanted to take any kind of risk he offered and throw caution to the wind. Luckily, though, they turned into the hospital drive, and she didn't have to continue trying to hide her tumble of conflicting thoughts.

"This is where I get out," she murmured, fumbling with the door.

Rick said nothing. He reached over to open Tracey's door, his face only inches from hers. His eyes looked deeply into her green depths. He was so close, she could smell the spicy scent of his aftershave. It invaded her senses and made her suddenly feel as if he was all around her, enveloping her with his willpower. All he had to do was move his face a few inches and he could kiss her. She was too stunned to stop her own mouth as it drifted toward his in a searching kiss. She felt all her nerve endings start to tingle and it was as if her heart was awakening for the first time. A kiss had never felt like this before. . . .

The sound of a car horn startled both of them. Rick turned around and saw a car behind them, wanting to pull up to the hospital entrance.

Tracey jerked the door open and almost jumped out of the car. She had to get out before she fell under his spell again and agreed to drive with him in the rally. "Thanks for the lift. If I don't see you, I'll send you word about Troy."

"Think over my offer, will you?" Rick's voice was husky and low. "We'd make a perfect team."

She flushed, but said nothing as she slammed the car door and walked toward the hospital emergency room. Eventually, she heard the roar of his engine as he drove away, but she resisted the impulse to look back at him.

Her legs were slightly wobbly as she reached the emergency room, and she could still feel her heart fluttering within her breast. What was wrong with her? She'd been kissing Rick in a hospital parking lot! Another rush of heated excitement coursed through her veins at the thought of them driving together—they would be a great team, she knew it.

Forget it! It was a fantasy that could never happen.

She took a couple of calming breaths as she entered the emergency room. She was here to see about Troy, and she needed to put Rick Masters out of her mind.

She looked around the room and immediately spotted her father, sitting in a chair, calmly reading a magazine.

"Tracey!" James Danvers exclaimed as he caught sight of his daughter's flaming hair out of the corner of his eye.

"How's Troy?" Tracey asked as she placed a comforting arm around her father's shoulders. He appeared composed, but Tracey noted the strain around his eyes.

"You'll see for yourself," he answered in mock exasperation. "All he can talk about is how stupid he was not to look where he was walking, how this is going to affect his racing, and on and on."

Tracey grinned. Her father wouldn't berate her twin so, if he hadn't actually been worried. But he also wouldn't go on like that if Troy weren't all right now.

"Is the doctor with him?"

He nodded. "They're taking a few more X-rays just to make sure nothing's been broken." He then leveled a steady gaze at his daughter. "You know, this means that Troy won't be able to drive with you in that rally."

Tracey kept her voice light. "I know, but it's only one race, and Troy's more important to me than some silly rally."

James gave his daughter an approving nod. "It's hard, I know, but you'll have another chance."

"I know that, Dad, but you've always said, 'People are more important.' " She squeezed her father's hand; then a mischievous smile appeared on her face. "But that's not going to stop me from giving Troy a hard time."

Tracey peeked behind the curtain of the emergency room only to see a young, pretty nurse joking with Troy as she finished bandaging his ankle. "Feeling much better, I see." Tracey's voice was laced with amusement as she carefully positioned herself on the side of the bed.

"Huh!" he protested in irritation. "Look at this! I can't believe it happened." He gestured at the offensive ankle in disgust.

"What actually caused the sprain? Jake said he didn't—"

"I'm too embarrassed to tell you." Troy hung his head dramatically. Then he glanced up sideways. "Okay. I'll tell. It was a stupid oil spill."

"How did oil—"

"It was left on the garage floor, and I slipped on it as I was coming around a corner."

Tracey's lips started to twitch in amusement. She couldn't laugh. It would annoy Troy even further. But the idea of him falling on something as silly as a puddle of oil was so ridiculous!

Troy eyed his sister suspiciously. "Don't you dare even think of laughing, Tracey. I feel awful enough as it is."

Tracey struggled to keep her face devoid of emotion.

"Just wait till I find out who left that engine oil on the garage floor," Troy threatened ominously.

"Just a few more minutes," the nurse interjected as she continued wrapping an elastic bandage around the ankle. Once she finished, she gave Troy one last long sweep of her eyelashes as she said softly: "You can leave now Mr. Danvers, but if that ankle troubles you, don't hesitate to call." She flashed him one last pointed look before she left.

"It *troubles* me to be such a jerk," Troy muttered once the nurse was out of earshot.

"You're acting like it's the end of the world," Tracey admonished.

He avoided her eyes almost guiltily. "It's the end of the rally."

"I know," she responded with a deliberately light tone.

Troy tilted his head to look gravely at his sister. "I'm sorry. I know how much this rally meant to you."

"No more than it meant to you."

"It meant a lot to both of us, and now I've ruined our chances."

"Look, it isn't the Daytona 500 or anything. It's just a little rally."

"But it would've been good publicity." Troy gave a little shrug of regret.

Tracey shifted uncomfortably. She couldn't let Troy wallow in this pool of self-pity since it might hinder his recovery. "I may be in the rally yet," Tracey informed him.

Troy looked blank. "You can't drive alone—"

"Who says I'm going alone? I've already had another offer."

"What? Who?" Troy demanded, his disgust over his ankle momentarily forgotten.

Tracey leaned back and tossed her hair over her shoulder saucily. "No one important—just Rick Masters."

"Rick Masters?" Troy exclaimed in disbelief.

Tracey nodded.

"Great! It's almost worth having sprained this stupid ankle."

Now it was Tracey's turn to be surprised. "Troy, you don't think I'm going to accept?"

"Why not? It's a great opportunity to learn from him. He's one of the best drivers around."

"There's nothing I want to learn from him," Tracey commented shortly.

"Who's learning what?" James Danvers asked as he pushed a wheelchair into Troy's room.

"Oh, nothing, Dad," Tracey answered hastily. "I

was just telling Troy that the rally isn't off yet, because I've had another offer.''

"Already?" he commented casually as he started to help Troy into the wheelchair.

"Do I have to ride in this thing?" Troy grated out in exasperation. "It's bad enough to have the sprain, but I feel like an invalid being wheeled around."

"Sorry, son, it's hospital rules," James explained patiently. "Stop grumbling. Sit back and enjoy the ride."

Once Troy was settled in the chair, he turned back to his sister with a glint in his eye. "Tell Dad who offered to drive in the rally with you," he prompted.

"No one really," she responded casually as she shot Troy a silencing look.

James looked up in curiosity. "Well?"

"It was Rick Masters."

"Excellent! What an opportunity for you," her father enthused.

Tracey groaned inwardly. Not only Troy, but now her father thought it was wonderful. Why had she ever mentioned it to her big-mouthed twin in the first place?

"When did you see him?"

"He gave me a ride here," Tracey said curtly. "But let's forget it, okay? I really wasn't even considering it."

James started to push the wheelchair down the hall and Tracey fell into step beside him. "Don't just dismiss the offer, Tracey. It's a way of still driving in the rally," he pointed out.

"I know, Dad, but I'm used to Troy. It would be

hard to drive with a complete stranger," Tracey tried to summon a plausible explanation.

"It's up to you, but think about it carefully," James warned her. "You may not get another opportunity."

Tracey's eyes clouded with uneasiness, as she felt torn inside. One part of her wanted to drive in the rally so badly and, if it had been anyone but Rick who offered, she would have probably jumped at the chance. But Rick. How could she agree to spend three days in his company? Three minutes and she seemed to lose all of her perspective. And if she grew to know him better, would she ever be able to compete against him as just another driver?

But, then again, maybe she'd get him out of her system if she drove in the rally with him. Maybe she'd see he was just another guy on the track, looking for a win any way he could get it.

Chapter Five

Rick stared down at the engine, trying to focus his eyes. He was weary, worn out. And still he wasn't finished. He rubbed the back of his neck, trying to ease the stiff muscles.

"Come on, man, let's give it a rest for a while," Skid said as he slapped Rick on the back. "There's nothing more we can do if we're falling over from lack of sleep."

Rick continued staring at the engine. "There's got to be something I've missed, something I've over-looked."

"Were you listening to me? Let it go, Rick."

Rick turned his head to confront the tired eyes of his crew chief. He felt guilty. He had driven them all to the point of exhaustion. They had to take a break. "Okay, just let me check—"

"No!" Skid pulled the hood of the car down and slammed it shut.

The slam of the hood snapped Rick out of his daze. "You're right. We'll break for breakfast and come back this afternoon."

Skid gave an exasperated snort. "Rick, we need sleep, not just a break. You haven't left this damn garage since you found out you weren't going to run in the rally. The rally is out, accept it.'' He continued in an encouraging tone. ''We'll have the car ready for the Daytona—that's the real issue, the point of all of this. The rally's nothing.''

Rick rubbed his eyes and leaned against the car. Skid made sense. It was ridiculous to push himself to the brink of exhaustion just because he was frustrated about the rally. Sure he'd wanted to run in it, but not just for publicity. Why? He didn't have to think twice. He wanted to be in it just to be close to Tracey. To see her red hair flying in the breeze, to watch her eyes light up with—

''Rick, phone call!'' one of the mechanics called from Jake's office.

''Right!'' He shouted back. Then he said to Skid: ''Jake will be coming in an hour or so, let's have him check it over one more time.''

Skid just nodded wearily.

''Masters here,'' Rick said into the telephone.

''It's Tracey Danvers.'' She felt an urge to hang up quickly, forget the whole idea.

There was silence for a few moments. Tracey could swear she could feel his smile from her end of the phone.

''Yes?''

She gritted her teeth. He wasn't going to let her off lightly. ''I was calling about our conversation a couple days ago. I've had a chance to think over your offer and I've decided to accept.''

''What offer was that?''

"You know what I mean!" she exclaimed. "The rally, of course."

"Oh, the rally."

There was silence again. Tracey took a deep breath. "So do you want to drive with me or not?" she asked him point blank.

"Do I have a choice?"

"A choice!" She almost laughed. "You were the one who suggested it."

She could hear him chuckling on the other end of the phone. "I was only teasing. Remember teasing? Something you did the first time we met."

"That was different. This is purely business," Tracey countered. "We're both getting what we want out of this arrangement."

"I agree." Rick tried to restrain the enthusiasm in his voice. He'd been ready to admit defeat—to rule the rally out. And now he'd be able not only to drive in it, but with Tracey. The corners of his mouth slowly turned up at the thought of being in the same car with her for three days.

"I'll meet you Monday morning at the check point. Come an hour before the rally starts."

"Right. See you then."

As Tracey hung up the phone, she bit her lip in indecision. Had she done the right thing? In just a week, it seemed as though Rick had turned her life upside down. And what was she doing now? Calling him to drive in the rally with her so she could spend three days exclusively in his company.

She reminded herself that she was a woman who

had learned the discipline and cool-headedness necessary to drive a car almost two hundred miles per hour; she certainly could control herself around one man—even one as handsome and magnetic as Rick.

Rick strolled back to his car, all his tiredness suddenly having disappeared. ''Skid, give the boys a break—I've got another offer to drive in the rally.''

''Great! We'll be able to keep your name in the public eye before Daytona,'' Skid enthused. ''Who? It can't be Carrera?''

''No. Tracey Danvers.'' Rick walked over to the lockers and started to unzip his grease-splattered overalls. ''Her brother was injured. So she needs a partner—and I need a car.''

''You're going to drive with a rookie?'' Skid exclaimed in disbelief.

''What's wrong with that?''

''Why waste your time? You want to win the rally, not nurse along a fledgling driver.''

Rick yanked off the overalls and tucked his shirt into his jeans. ''I think we can win. I've seen her drive and she's not bad—a little ragged around the edges, but maybe I can help her along.''

Skid's mouth gaped opened in amazement. ''Help her! You've got to *beat* her. What's the matter with you, Rick? She's your competition.''

Rick was trying to control his temper. He liked Skid, they'd had a profitable partnership together, but this was *his* decision. ''I'm well aware of that, but the rally is just publicity—you said that yourself.''

Skid's eyes narrowed suspiciously. "Wait a minute, pal, you're not interested in her, are you?"

Rick was combing his hair, looking into the small mirror fixed above the lockers. "If I am, it's my business," he said in a clipped voice. He saw the image of Tracey in his mind, her face, suddenly vulnerable, turned up to his as he kissed her in the car.

"It's *my* business if it starts interfering with your driving," Skid said. "Remember why we came here, Rick. You and I have a goal—and nothing can interfere with that."

Still looking in the mirror, the image of Tracey faded as Rick's eyes strayed to his scar. "Don't worry, I won't forget it. I came here to win."

Two days later, Tracey pulled the Thunderbird pace car that had been mocked up to resemble her stock car into the line of other rally cars. Most of them were already in place at the Daytona International Speedway where the race was scheduled to begin.

As she looked around at some of the early arrivals, there was no sign of Rick. A quick and disturbing thought occurred to her: maybe he wouldn't even show up. She hadn't heard from him all weekend and now she wondered if he had any intention of driving with her at all. No, he had to show up, she reminded herself. He wanted to be in the rally as much as she did.

Tracey got out of the pace car and stretched her long legs. No use getting cramped when she would be in there almost exclusively for the next three days.

She saw Paco Carrera, who was three cars up, wave

to her. She smiled and waved back. Engines were revving, people were shouting and laughing, but Tracey just couldn't seem to relax. Take it easy, she cautioned herself. Her first big win was just around the corner.

As she rotated her neck to loosen the muscles, she looked down at the comfortable clothing she had chosen. It was hardly glamorous, but, after hours behind the wheel, glamor would be the last thing on her mind. She had dressed for ease of movement with loose green sweatpants, a white tee-shirt, and a light green jacket. Her high-top sneakers were practical as well, since her ankles needed the support during the day. She had deliberately fastened her red hair into a simple ponytail. She meant business, and she wanted Rick to see that she knew what she was doing. She wasn't here to attract him—just to win the rally.

A little voice inside of her, however, told her that attracting him *and* winning the rally was the ideal combination.

Thirty minutes later, Tracey was drumming her fingers on the hood of her car. She checked her watch again. Where was Rick? He was supposed to be here half an hour ago. She felt the perspiration break out across her forehead. Impatiently, she whipped off her jacket. The morning sun was already starting to heat up the raceway. But it was more than the heat bothering her; her nerves were all keyed up that Rick might not show up.

Maybe he'd had second thoughts. Why would he want to drive with her when he could easily find an-

other, more experienced partner? Maybe he'd realized—

"Going somewhere, Tracey?" Rick asked from the
other side of the car.

Tracey felt relief rush through her. He was here. At
last, he was here.

As she turned around, she watched his ruggedly
handsome face break into a slight, crooked smile.
"Didn't you think I'd be here?"

She pointed at her watch. "You're late. I don't like
cutting it too close."

"Me either, but I had to pick up a few things," he
responded smoothly as he stowed two large bags into
the back of the car.

"What is all of that?" she asked.

He casually walked around to her side of the car.
"A surprise. Something to keep us entertained after a
long day on the road."

Tracey felt a tiny thrill run through her. What type
of "entertainment" was he talking about? No, she
didn't want to know. It was hard enough to be in the
same car with him, without speculating about how they
would spend their evenings at the rally stop points. "I
thought we agreed to keep this on an impersonal level."

"Ground rules?"

"Right. It's a long three days."

With an unexpected touch of his hand, he tilted her
face up slightly. "And I'm looking forward to every
minute."

She looked into his grey eyes, only inches from her,
and felt a warmth flow through her as she saw the

twinkle there. It was reserved for her alone, and that made her absurdly happy.

He stroked her chin lightly. "And I'm sure you won't mind if I drive first."

Tracey pulled her chin away sharply. So that's what he was after with the come-on! "I do mind. It's my pace car, and I'll drive first." She might have known he was up to something with his teasing compliments. The first driver was always considered the premiere driver, and she wanted that prestige.

"But you wouldn't be driving in the rally if it weren't for me being part of your team," he countered.

She sighed in frustration; then an idea occurred to her. "Okay, since we can't agree, let's flip a coin. Heads you drive first; tails I drive first."

He nodded in agreement.

Tracey pulled a coin out of her pocket and said a little prayer over it before she tossed it in the air.

As she caught the coin and flipped it over her hand, she looked down at it: heads.

Rick patted her shoulder lightly. "Sorry, Tracey, but it's the 'flip of the coin', so to speak."

She frowned at his joviality. Of course, he could afford to be amused; he had won. Shoot! What a way to start the rally. If it had been Troy he would have let her start without the slightest hesitation—Troy always let her take the lead.

"Shall we get ready? Five minutes till start-up," Rick tossed off over his shoulder as he threw the rest of his gear into the back of the car.

Tracey said nothing. She simply walked over to the

passenger side and eased herself into the car. As she settled down and strapped herself in, she fumed silently. Rick had the devil's own luck.

He slid in beside her, and she was aware of his brief glance at her. Then she heard the loudspeaker announce: "Ladies and gentlemen, start your engines, please."

Rick flipped the key in the ignition, bringing the Thunderbird engine roaring into life. He then shifted the car into gear and began to maneuver up to the starting position. Once they reached their place, an official in a striped racing shirt came over to their car.

"Danvers team?" the short, balding man asked as he leaned toward the driver's window.

"Yes, but I'm driving for Troy Danvers," Rick explained. "Rick Masters."

Tracey watched the man's glance sharpen with interest. "*The* Rick Masters?"

Rick nodded.

"A pleasure to meet you, sir," his voice was filled with obvious admiration. "And I hope you enjoy our rally."

"I'm sure we both will," Tracey interjected as she leaned over to Rick's side of the car.

"A woman?" he said to Rick.

"Yes, and I'm also driving," Tracey cut in, trying to keep the sarcasm out of her voice.

The man gave a smile of disbelief, and then continued in an official tone. "You know the rules. No going over the posted speed limit. The route is up to you, but no interstate travel. Cars gain points for arrival time at each destination check-in. The car with the most points at the end of the three days wins. Got it?''

''Right,'' Rick said.

''Here's your map. See you in Pensacola tonight.'' The man handed Rick the map of the destinations where they were supposed to stop, and then walked over to the next car.

''I guess we're all set.'' Rick handed the map to Tracey, who yanked it out of his hand. It wasn't his fault that he was famous, but it still rankled that the official dismissed her so easily.

A few minutes later, the starting gun fired and the cars roared into life, each taking what its driver considered to be the fastest route to Ocala, their first check-in point.

As Rick drove the Thunderbird out of the International Speedway, he looked over at Tracey. ''Am I still getting the silent treatment?'' he inquired.

''I'm not being silent. I've nothing to say.'' Tracey folded her arms across her chest in a dismissive gesture.

''What about our route to Ocala? Any suggestions?''

She eyed him warily. ''Are you going to treat me as a full member of this team?''

''I always intended to,'' he answered. ''If it's bothering you, I can't help that I won the coin toss. And I can't help it if that guy back there was a jerk.''

Tracey grudgingly admitted to herself that this was true. ''Okay, then we work together all the way.''

He reached over and caught her hand. It felt so soft. Instantly, the contact made his heart beat with the pulse of music as his flesh met hers in a warm clasp. "Partners?" That word had a nice ring to it.

"At least for this rally." Tracey started as she felt his strong fingers close over hers. His hand was lean and strong—the hand of a driver. A surge of warmth ran through her at the touch of his fingers. Somehow it felt so right—the way her hand fit with his, as if they belonged together. Abruptly, she stopped this train of thought and pulled her hand away. She then picked up the map and pretended to study it intently.

"I think we should take State Road 40 to Ocala," she suggested. "I know that road and it's the fastest."

"I agree," Rick concurred. He made a couple of left turns, and soon they were on the road that would take them to Ocala.

Tracey watched the semi-tropical foliage grow more dense as they moved farther away from the Daytona Beach area. In the last ten years, it seemed as though the area had exploded, not only with tourists but year-round residents. She wondered where it would stop.

"Have you lived in Daytona all your life?" Rick broke into her thoughts.

Tracey smiled and leaned her head back against the seat. The wind was blowing across her face, whipping up stray strands of hair. "All my life. I grew up on the beach, but it sure has changed."

"Did you always want to race cars?" he asked, keeping his eyes straight ahead.

"Always. I can't think of a time when I didn't want to race." She smiled in remembrance. "When I was just a little girl, Dad would take me on the back roads and I'd sit on his lap and drive the car. That was just the beginning.''

One black brow lifted slightly. "You have to admit it's an unusual occupation for a woman."

Her green eyes narrowed slightly as she looked at his profile. "What's so unusual about it?"

"Well, for one, the danger."

"Don't you think that women dream of the same type of adventure that men do? That we might want the same thrill of taking on a speeding race car and winning?" Her voice grew passionate.

"I can't say that I've given it any thought," he commented, but with one look at her mutinous face, he added hastily: "But I agree—if you want adventure, gender shouldn't hold you back. I wouldn't be in this car with you, if I didn't think that."

Tracey relaxed again. "We agree then."

"What does your mother have to say? Isn't she worried about you?"

"She died when I was just a baby," Tracey responded without emotion. She looked over at Rick's stilled features. "It's okay. I really don't remember her at all. She's just a picture to me. It would've been nice though—" she left the sentence unfinished. In the last few days, she had been missing having a mother more than ever. She needed to talk to someone about Rick, have a mother to open up to about the mysteries of her feelings for him. Tracey gave a little sigh. "But, if she were here, I think she'd approve. She loved racing and she loved my father."

"And your father?"

"Dad always encouraged me to drive as Troy's equal. Troy didn't want to drive professionally, but I did."

Rick felt the sadness in her voice, even though she tried to hide it. She'd grown up in a man's world and had to establish her independence at an early age. He wanted to reach out and gently place her head against his shoulder—let her be vulnerable with him. "Is that when James stopped driving? When your mother died?"

She shot a quick glance at him. "I know what you're thinking—he made his dream mine. But Dad was ready to stop racing. He'd had so many injuries. Mother's death was just the last straw."

In spite of her quick response, Tracey felt like he'd hit a raw nerve. It wasn't as though she hadn't asked herself that same question.

"Luckily, he raised another generation of race car drivers," Rick added lightly.

"But only because Troy and I showed interest at an early age," Tracey protested.

"And he didn't influence you to take on his dream?"

"No."

"Nor his ambitions?"

"They're mine, too."

"They are now."

"They always have been." Tracey could feel herself tightening inside. "Why the third degree? Do I have to justify myself?"

Rick shook his head. "Not to me. But those are

probably the questions you're going to hear from reporters—you'll need to be able to answer them."

"I see," Tracey said slowly. "So this is part of the
tutoring process—How to Handle the Media 101?"

A flash of humor crossed his face, bringing out the
crinkles around his eyes. "Okay, I deserved that. But
once you start winning, you'd better be prepared for
some tough questions."

Tracey's confidence spiraled upward as she heard
the word "winning." So Rick felt she would be winning? And soon. Her delight grew as she realized that
he believed in her, even if he hadn't said so in so many
words.

"Oh no!" her smile suddenly faded.

"What?" Rick's hands tightened on the wheel.

"It's Paco!" She pointed at the bright green Chevy
Illumina stalled on the side of the road. Smoke was
billowing out from the under the hood of the car; Paco
Carrera was shouting and gesturing frantically at his
driving partner.

"Already?" Rick questioned, though he didn't turn
his head even for a few seconds to look at the disabled
car. "We're only a few miles from the first check point
in Ocala."

Tracey looked around in surprise at the rolling hills
signaling the horse country of central Florida. She'd
been so caught up in their conversation, she hadn't
kept track of how far they'd come, or if any other rally
drivers were pacing with them.

"What about Paco?"

"Not much we can do," Rick said as he pressed the

gas pedal down a fraction more. "His bad luck still seems to be dogging him."

"Poor Paco."

Rick tossed her an ironic look. "Don't feel too sorry for him."

"And why not?" she inquired. "He's a fellow driver. I'd hate to see him go out so early in the rally."

"He takes his chances like the rest of us," Rick reminded her. "There can only be one winner, Tracey. You'd better remember that. We compete against each other all the time."

Tracey's features tightened imperceptively, her buoyant mood fading. Was he trying to warn her that they shouldn't get too comfortable with each other because they'd have to keep that competitive edge? She knew it was true. If she couldn't deliver, she'd find herself like Paco—without sponsorship, doing anything to get a contract to drive for someone. "Thanks for the advice again," she emphasized the last word ironically. "But I know the facts."

"I'm not even going to touch that one," Rick said drily. Then, in a serious tone, he added, "You know, there's nothing wrong with admitting you've got something to learn."

"Who did you learn from?" She decided to change tactics.

"Anyone who'd teach me—I was as green as they come when I first started racing," Rick's eyes seemed to see down a different road than the one before him. "I had to learn from the ground up."

"What about your parents?"

His features seemed to harden. ''Unlike yours—they were totally against my racing career.''

Tracey's jade eyes widened to search his profile. ''What do they think now?''

''They're both dead,'' Rick said shortly.

Tracey felt the tension in his body. His parents' attitude about his profession was something that obviously still rankled. ''What did you do all those years when you weren't racing?'' she asked gently.

He smiled in self-mockery. ''All those years? I'm not over the hill yet.''

''I wasn't suggesting—''

''I know,'' he cut in. His voice grew reflective. ''I spent a lot of time making money so I could do what I wanted someday, which turned out to be—surprise— racing. But I guess I never really stopped thinking or dreaming about it.'' How could he tell her he relived his accident over and over in his dreams until he was driven almost half-crazy? How that one turn haunted him—the one that had been the end of everything.

''Once it gets into your system, you can't get it out,'' Tracey quipped.

Rick grinned in agreement. ''We're a lot alike.''

Tracey was silent. Maybe not. She could still smell the rancid smoke from Paco's car. If that had been Rick broken down on the road, would she have just driven past him without a backward glance?

''Aren't you going to ask?''

''What?''

''Why I stopped racing.''

''I just assumed it was—''

''The crash? That was part of it—''

''You're the first car!'' a man shouted at them as they were greeted by a dozen or so cheering people. He clocked their time and wrote down the number of the car. ''You must've been making excellent time.''

''It seemed to go by quickly, thanks to my companion,'' Rick responded.

''Lucky you.'' The man took in Tracey's flaming hair and lissome figure.

''I'm his co-driver, if you're interested,'' Tracey added with a saccharine smile.

''Of course.'' The man winked at Rick, a gesture not lost on Tracey.

''Just check us in,'' Tracey retorted.

The man handed them the check-in card with their number of points. ''See you in Pensacola.''

Rick put the car into gear and sped back out toward the highway.

''Day one—and we're already leading,'' Tracey almost sang out as she fanned herself with the check-in card.

''We're setting the pace. Tomorrow will be the challenge to hold on to it,'' Rick reminded her.

''I know,'' Tracey was slightly sobered. ''But I'm going to enjoy it while it lasts.''

As she watched Rick accelerate onto the highway, Tracey had to concede that he was an excellent driver. His eyes were always moving, assessing everything around the car; his speed was constant and steady. Of course, rally driving couldn't even compare with the grueling type of track events that he usually drove in, but she was impressed.

For the next three hours she waited for him to explain why he stopped racing, but he didn't bring up the subject again. He talked about the Darlington and Phoenix races he won the last few months and some of the driving techniques he used, but the conversation remained superficial. The moment had passed.

Get him out of your mind! It's his life. You've got other things to concentrate on.

Rick kept his mind on the road and racing. He had to concentrate. Being in this car with Tracey made it seem like they were the only two people in the world. The intimacy made him want to share feelings he didn't know he had, and come to realizations about his life he wasn't ready to make. Just her presence made him happy. Every time she turned her head, he caught the glimmer of her hair out of the corner of his eye and he had to grimly remind himself to keep his eyes on the road.

It didn't make him feel tense; it was sweet agony.

It was well past sunset when they arrived in Pensacola. A small crowd had gathered and they clapped enthusiastically as Rick and Tracey roared past the marker. As they climbed out of the Thunderbird, several photographers started snapping pictures.

"You're the first, and what a first!" one of the photographers shouted as he coaxed a smile out of Tracey. He clicked some pictures of her. "Some great driving, guys."

"We're a team. Make sure you put that down,"

Rick reminded him. He then placed an arm around Tracey for a photograph.

Her eyes sparkled as she faced the camera with Rick by her side. She felt a tremor pass through her as his warm hand pressed against her shoulder. They were a team—at least for today.

Chapter Six

"See you later for dinner?" Rick asked as they checked in.

She started to decline, but, as she stole a glance at his face, his eyes seemed to flicker with eager expectation—making her heart soar. "Thanks, I'd like that. I'll meet you here around nine."

Once Tracey was in her room, she stretched out on the bed and felt the tension drain away. It wasn't so much being in the car that length of time—she'd been in races that lasted over four hours—but it was being in the car with Rick. She was aware of his presence every minute. And it would be worse tomorrow because she would be driving. How would she ever be able to concentrate?

She rolled over and buried her face in the pillow. Think about that tomorrow, she told herself. It might not be that bad. Minutes later, she drifted off into a dreamless sleep.

Later, Tracey awoke feeling slightly disoriented. As she looked at her watch, she realized she had slept two hours and now only had thirty minutes before she had to meet Rick for dinner. She jumped off the bed and raced into the shower.

101

As she was drying her flame-colored hair, her thoughts drifted back to the conversation she and Rick had shared in the car today. He seemed to reveal little about his past, except that his parents were dead and that neither of them had approved of his career choice. But why? And why had he stopped racing. Was the accident really the key? It just didn't make sense. He was not the type of man to be defeated easily. Underneath that easygoing charm was a man with nerves of steel and a will to match. He wouldn't have given up racing easily.

She looked at herself in the mirror with a little ironic grin.

I've got to stop trying to make the pieces of the Rick Masters puzzle fit together. It's his life. After this rally, I won't even see him again—except at races.

Trying to ignore the tug of depression at that thought, Tracey walked back into the bedroom, and pulled out the dress she had bought especially for the trip. When she had been shopping, she told herself it was just because she needed some new clothes, but, in the back of her mind, she knew she wanted to look good because Rick would be with her. She slipped a soft gauzy dress over her head and then pulled it down to where it settled, just below the knee. The saleswoman had said the copper color brought out amber highlights in her red hair, but as Tracey peered in the mirror, she wasn't sure she could see any. She added long, dangling copper earrings that tinkled pleasantly as she turned her head.

As she slipped on her metallic sandals, she started

to smile. She'd developed more interest in clothes in the last two weeks than she had in her entire life. At least Rick didn't know that she rarely wore a dress— so he wouldn't rib her as unmercifully as her twin.

When she met Rick downstairs, she saw that he too had changed into something more formal. He wore grey pants and a snowy white shirt with a thin grey stripe. His hair was still damp and a few sable tendrils hung over his forehead. It gave him a boyishly attractive look, making Tracey want to reach out and softly brush those errant locks back.

''Where's that grease monkey I've been driving with all day?'' Rick asked jokingly, but his eyes bathed her in admiration. How could she be in a car all day and look this fresh and pretty.

''I left her in the garage tonight—with the pace car.'' Tracey tilted her head back and smiled. ''So where do you want to have dinner?''

Rick's mind went blank as he looked down into those magical green eyes. What did it matter where they went as long he could watch her by candlelight and listen to her soft, musical voice.

''Well?'' Tracey prompted.

''Dinner—right,'' Rick blurted out, trying to clear his head. ''I thought maybe the historical district in Seville Square.''

Tracey nodded. ''Great. We can get away from the racing crowd for a while.'' But she didn't know if she wanted to get away from the other rally drivers or not. Being alone with Rick could be even more of a challenge. While they had been in the car during the day,

Tracey had been preoccupied with getting to their destination. But now there was just Rick and her—with the whole of an evening before them. She sternly reminded herself that they had to keep their arrangement purely on a business footing—even friendship could be dangerous to her fulfilling her dream.

But the word "friend" had such a nice ring. She'd never really been close with anyone outside her family. Even Roger had never been a friend—there was always a strained distance between the two of them. And she'd never been tempted to share her innermost feelings with him the way she was with Rick.

Tracey shivered slightly, not knowing whether it was from fear or anticipation.

Once they reached Seville Square in the heart of old Pensacola, they slowly walked through the streets lined with museums and historical houses.

"Have you been here before?" Rick asked, breaking the silence.

"It seems odd, being a Florida native—but no."

Rick smiled. "No race track here, right?"

Tracey flashed a grin at him.

"It's too bad we didn't arrive earlier. Most of the museums and houses are closed now. They're worth a visit."

"You've been here before?" Tracey couldn't help asking.

Rick gazed at her with a bland half-smile. "You could say that. My dad was stationed here at the Naval Air Station when he was in the navy."

"What?" Tracey exclaimed. "You lived in Pensacola?"

"For a few years—I lived *everywhere* for a few years." Rick's voice was laced with irony. "We moved around a lot. I lived in Alaska, the Philippines, California; you name it, and we were probably there."

"It must've been hard on you as a kid—moving around so much," Tracey said. She imagined a lonely, restless Rick as a young boy. Her fingers reached out and laced with his.

"It wasn't bad. Really. I had the chance to see some interesting corners of the world," Rick reflected, as he squeezed her hand in reassurance. "When I was a teenager, though, I wanted to be in the States and, by that time, I'd discovered racing."

"But you went to college here, didn't you?" Tracey asked before she could stop herself. She mentally kicked herself—why couldn't she learn to keep her mouth shut? She didn't want Rick to know that she had read every bio on him she could find.

Rick managed a choking laugh. "You could say that. But if you looked at my transcript, you'd know I spent all my time at the race track. I got my engineering degree by the skin of my teeth, Tracey."

"I was hardly the model student myself," she added. "I thought all that theory was a waste of time—I just wanted to be there working on engines."

"Looks like we have something else in common— we don't like academics."

"But you've read poetry," she reminded him gently.

"True. But not in school—on my own. My mother

taught English on the bases where we lived. She instilled a love of literature in me.''

''It didn't reflect in your grades, though,'' she commented in a light voice. But her eyes gleamed with a bright intensity. The thought of Rick reading poetry charmed her. What other sides of himself would he reveal to her? This was not a one-dimensional man. He had depth and sensitivity.

She shivered again, but, in spite of her thoughts, this time it was from the temperature. Northern Florida was not as warm as Daytona, and there was a distinct chill in the air now that evening had set in.

''Would you like my jacket?'' Rick asked, immediately noting her discomfort.

Tracey shook her head. She had to remain alert. If she became too comfortable with Rick, she might forget why they had originally agreed to team up for the rally.

''Is this all right?'' Rick halted their progress and gestured at the menu in the window of the Spanish-styled, stuccoed Alhambra restaurant. ''I know the food is good and the atmosphere quiet. At least it was years ago.''

''Lovely.''

As they walked in, Rick's face fell in almost comic dismay. Instead of the serene Spanish ambiance he remembered, the restaurant seemed to have more activity than pit row on the race track. It wasn't just noisy; it was bursting at the seams with loud-voiced customers. Rushing waiters dashed by with trays filled to capacity, and a much harried maitre d' eyed them warily.

"A little crowded tonight?" Tracey joked, trying to relieve the tension. She was rewarded by a look of hatred from the maitre d'.

"It's this rally," he explained through tightly compressed lips. "Everyone decided to come here for dinner. Without reservations, I might add."

Tracey and Rick exchanged guilty looks. "We'll try some place else," Rick offered. He took Tracey's arm and steered her back to the door, when they heard a voice shout, "Rick Masters! Over here!"

Slowly, they turned around to see Paco Carrera motioning to them from his table.

Tracey eyed Rick with an apologetic glance. "I guess we don't have much of a choice," she said reluctantly.

"It would be rude, since the last time we saw him he was standing on the side of the road with a steaming engine," Rick reminded her, but the mischievous glint in his grey eyes belied his serious tone. "And don't forget The Trackside when you left him in the middle of the dance floor."

Tracey's cheeks flushed as her thoughts drifted back to the dance floor at The Trackside. "You were the one who cut in," she hissed.

"But only because I knew you wanted me to."

"I did not!" Tracey protested.

"Are you or are you not going to join your friend?" the maitre d' interrupted in an exasperated voice.

"We'll be joining him, thank you," Tracey tried to answer with as much dignity as she could summon.

As Tracey and Rick approached the table, she noticed that Paco was by himself. Everyone else seemed to be overflowing with fun and laughter, but Paco had his head propped up with one hand and a distinctly morose look on his face. She exchanged a warning look with Rick. He gave a what-can-I-do? shrug as he held the chair out for her.

Any hope of a pleasant dinner was immediately dispelled by Paco's first remark: "I guess you know what happened today." He hung his head dejectedly.

Tracey flashed Rick a threatening look as his mouth started to twitch slightly. "Not really," she said. "We saw you a few miles out of Ocala—thought you had engine trouble."

"Engine trouble!" he spat out. "The damned thing blew a gasket before I was even to the halfway point."

"Bad luck, that's for sure," Rick sympathized. "My own pace car blew a piston before the race even started and they couldn't replace it in time."

She shot him a grateful look; then turned back to Paco. "It was bad luck, but today was just the first day of the rally," she tried to reassure him.

"No, bad luck is the name of the game for me—it's been bad since the Darlington race last year." He looked pointedly at Rick.

"Look, man, you can't blame me. We drove a clean race, and I just happened to have won." Rick's voice was firm, but compassionate.

"But you can't deny that race started my run of car problems."

Rick shrugged. "Who doesn't have car problems? These are high performance engines; there's always something going wrong with them. You're lucky if your car actually makes it through a race. You know that."

"It's true," Tracey agreed. "This thing about bad luck—that's just superstition."

Paco was shaking his head. "Not the kind of problems I've had—it's more than just losing. It's almost like a curse."

Tracey glanced at Rick, expecting him to show impatience with Paco's self-pity but, instead, his dark brows were drawn together in thoughtful concentration. She smiled a little. Rick might drive like god in his chariot, and drive to win, but he did have feeling for his fellow racers. "What kind of problems?" Tracey asked gently.

Paco's eyes gleamed, and instantly Tracey knew she'd made a mistake asking him that question. He promptly launched into a discussion detailing his engine problems through their appetizers, lamenting over his tire blowouts during their entrees, and grousing about his ignition failures over their desserts.

By the time Tracey was sipping her after-dinner coffee, she wondered if he would ever stop droning on. She felt like screaming after the first hour, and now she was almost in a daze. She sympathized with his problems, but enough was enough.

It certainly wasn't how she had imagined her evening

with Rick. Her eyes clouded with the vision of how it should have been: an intimate, quiet dinner with soft candlelight and the subtle strains of music in the background. Rick would have told her more about himself and she—

"Tracey, I don't think you heard Paco's question," Rick interrupted her thoughts. "He wanted to know if you've modified your restrictor plates."

Tracey could have strangled Paco. The least he could do is let her dream about how wonderful Rick's and her dinner could have been. Something inside of her seemed to snap. She couldn't take one more minute of this conversation and, in fact, was surprised at Rick's patience.

She stood up abruptly. "I think I've had enough shop-talk tonight, Paco."

Rick jumped up immediately—grateful for the chance to get them both out of there. "We've got to get an early start."

Paco's eyes raked them both. "Right. You're the point leaders—at least until tomorrow night," he added.

"We intend to keep it that way," Rick promised with a hint of steel in his voice. He wasn't going to let Paco intimidate Tracey—they were going to win this rally as a team.

Rick turned and guided Tracey out of the restaurant. Once they were outside, their eyes met for a few moments of silence. Suddenly, they both burst into laughter.

"I don't know how you could be so patient," Tracey

murmured, half-laughing, half-crying. "He went on the entire evening!"

Rick grimaced in good humor. "It wasn't easy. But strange as it sounds, I respect Paco. He's a good driver; he's just down on his luck."

"I know, believe me, I know," Tracey added with an exaggerated emphasis in her voice.

"You don't think I'm just a cold-hearted competitor now?" Rick asked.

She gazed up at him speculatively, barely making out his strong features in the evening shadows. "I think there's more compassion in you than you're willing to show."

There was a spark of some indefinable emotion that passed between them. Rick's voice deepened to a husky whisper. "Maybe you bring that out in me. I don't know if I would've sat there all evening and listened to him if you hadn't been with me."

Tracey felt breathless. "I don't want to take away your competitive edge."

She saw a flash of white teeth in the darkness. "No chance. No one does that, not even you."

The hard edge of his voice was belied by the warm touch of his hands on her arms. She felt his fingers burn into her skin where they gripped her almost too tightly. She swayed toward him, drawn by the vitality that radiated from his being. She wanted to feel the magic of his kiss again, the swirling of emotion between them that made her forget that when the rally was over, they would go back to being competitors.

His head started to slowly bend toward her, and she

turned her face up to him, when the door to the restaurant opened and several rally drivers came swaggering out.

"Hey, you two!" a loud voice mocked. "You've got an early start tomorrow. Let's see if you can hold your lead!"

Rick's hands slowly ran down her arms. "We'll hold on to it all right," Rick shouted back good-naturedly, his eyes still on Tracey.

"Let's get out of here," Tracey whispered.

Rick nodded. He took her hand in his and they strolled in silence back to the hotel. But Rick's mind was far from quiet. What was happening between the two of them? It wasn't just that he wanted to kiss her a few moments ago. He did. But he also just wanted to be with her, enjoy the easy comraderie they seemed to have fallen into over the course of the day. He'd never really been close to anyone. He'd always been a loner. But now he could see what it meant to have a partner—if only for the rally.

When they reached Tracey's room, she turned to Rick, her features deceptively composed. "I'll see you in the morning then."

His eyes searched her face, reaching into her thoughts. "I'm sorry the evening turned out the way it did."

A flash of humor crossed her face. "It wasn't what either of us expected."

Rick tenderly lifted a strand of her silky hair. "I've come to expect the unexpected when I'm with you.

Ever since that day at the track, nothing's gone as planned.''

Tracey stiffened. ''I don't understand.''

''Yes, you do. We can't let this partnership thing get any further out of control. You want to win, and I—'' he seemed to struggle for words.

''What?''

''I . . . have to drive with you,'' he paused as he let the strand of hair slip through his fingers. ''And then against you.''

Tracey felt an instant's squeezing hurt at his words. It was true. She couldn't let herself get carried away during this rally and lose sight that their team was just a matter of convenience for both of them. She cleared her throat that felt suspiciously tight and said in a bright voice: ''You're right, we're both too smart to let anything distract us from our goals.''

They both turned away from each other. When Tracey had gone into her room and closed the door, Rick looked back. What was he doing? What was ''smart'' about letting a woman like Tracey go? Did he want to win that much? He clenched his hand into a fist, ready to knock, but stopped himself. He couldn't ruin it for her. She had to keep herself clear of any emotional entanglements, so she could focus on winning. She had to have her chance. He couldn't take that away from her. Rick turned on his heel and resolutely walked away.

The next morning, Tracey awoke early and was checking over the Thunderbird pace car long before anyone else from the rally had made an appearance. She had slept fitfully, dreaming one bizarre sequence after another of Rick racing next to her, trying to drive her off the track; then he was embracing her, holding her against his heart.

Eventually, she had given up on trying to get any decent rest, and decided to use her time more productively: She checked over every part of her car that could possibly cause a problem on the road. She thought that her mind would be free of Rick if she checked and rechecked valves and hoses.

But she was wrong. She kept thinking of how she had stood on her side of the door in her room last night, listening to Rick's breathing on the other side. She waited to see if he would knock—and if he had—she would've known that he wanted her friendship more than anything. But he hadn't. Something had made him turn away. That something was the International Raceway that stretched between them like a vast desert. He couldn't afford to let himself get tangled up with a rookie. He obviously had his own game plan and that didn't include her.

She slammed the hood down.

"The rally doesn't start for another two hours," Rick said from behind her.

"No time like the present," Tracey responded without even looking around. She knew whose voice it was—those deep, rich sounds were burned into her brain.

"Are you anticipating any problems?" he asked quietly.

Tracey started to brush past him to retrieve the tire pressure gauge. ''There's always a possibility.''

Rick grasped her arm. ''Couldn't sleep, either?'' His glance held her steadily, and she noticed faint rings under his metallic grey eyes. The slight black stubble on his jaw made him look as if he'd had a restless night, too.

''Must be the excitement of the rally,'' Tracey murmured as she tried to pull her arm away. She wouldn't admit that he was haunting her dreams as well as her waking hours.

Rick tightened his fingers, rubbing the sensitive skin of her inner arm with his thumb. ''We had just about all the excitement we could take last night—with Paco.'' Rick had a suspicious tilt to the corners of his mouth.

Tracey couldn't help herself as a smile broke through her mask of uncertainty. ''It wasn't all that bad—just different.''

''How did you expect it to turn out?'' His words were playful, but the meaning was not. He wanted to know.

''Oh, the usual, of course,'' Tracey kept her tone deliberately nonchalant. ''Candlelight, wine, and a big romantic kiss at the end of the evening, as we gazed up at the moonlight and the stars from the back of your famous Grand Prix.''

Rick's fingers stopped their movements and he stared at her. Then his rich laughter rippled through the air. ''Now that would be a neat trick since my stock car is back in Daytona and doesn't have a back seat.''

"Exactly."

"Perhaps we could—"

"Not on your life," she cut him off.

Rick's eyes glowed in appreciation of her humor. He loved her comebacks—they tickled him. "I don't know. With a few modifications. . . . "

"Okay, let's get serious." Tracey handed him a checklist. "We need to go over each item. I don't want us to end up like Paco did yesterday."

"If we did get stranded, it would give us a chance to explore that backseat idea," Rick suggested on a hopeful note.

"Rick!"

"All right." He gave an exaggerated sigh. "I'll check the tires."

Chapter Seven

" "Let's take highway 10 back through Tallahassee, and . . . ," Rick paused as he scanned the map. "Then 19 south to St. Petersburg—the check-in point. That road isn't a major highway, but I think we can make better time."

Tracey kept her eyes on the road. "Sounds good to me. You're navigating today." She felt confident and in control now that she was behind the wheel. If she was able to keep her speed constant, they might be able to stay ahead on day two of the rally. That only left the stretch between Sanibel Island and Key West tomorrow.

"This is a new experience for me—letting someone else drive," Rick commented as he eyed her profile appreciatively. He hadn't noticed before how her nose tipped up slightly at the end. Or how her smooth skin glowed with gold undertones. Everything about her was beginning to fascinate him. "But there're definitely some advantages to being a passenger."

"You can watch the scenery."

Rick turned his face toward the window. "Oh, yeah, the Florida landscape—it's beautiful, too."

Tracey felt her cheeks grow warm at the compliment.

Somehow he made her feel feminine, in spite of the green sweatpants and functional tee-shirt. Her hands probably smelled of oil, too, since she had checked the oil and filter only half an hour ago. But Rick didn't seem to mind at all. Her hands flexed on the wheel. Keep your mind on the race, she reminded herself. Scenery. That's a safe topic. "Actually, I think this part of the state looks more like Georgia than Florida."

Rick's eyes scanned the flat, rolling hills, dotted with pine trees. "It's sure different from Los Angeles."

"Do you miss California?"

"Well . . . it was the longest I've ever been in one place," Rick answered. "I told you how we moved around when I was a kid. We were never in one place for very long. Then, when I got into racing, it seems like I just kept drifting from track to track."

"When Mom died, Dad bought the house in California. I guess the moving around finally got to him, too," Rick continued.

"Is that when you had the crash?" Tracey asked softly. There was a new, deep note in Rick's voice. She sensed he was sharing feelings from the heart.

Rick nodded. "I went to stay with my dad while I recuperated. For once, I had a place to call home. And Dad and I finally started to connect. Maybe that was one of the reasons I wasn't too anxious to start racing after the crash—I finally had a home."

"But then Dad died, and six months later I met Skid." Rick paused. "There didn't seem much to keep me in California, so I got back into racing."

"Regrets?"

"No, I don't think so," Rick answered slowly. "I had unfinished business on the Daytona Raceway. But I feel like I'm drifting again. I guess you never know what's going to be around the next turn."

Silence descended in the car. Tracey reached out and lay her hand over his. "Especially if you take it too high," she added playfully, wanting to clear those shadows from Rick's eyes.

Rick flashed her a quick smile. How could he tell her that she took away that aching need in him to find something permanent? He didn't know how, but she managed to make him feel like it was possible to find what he'd been looking for. "Okay, Miss Anonymous Fan, how would you take Turn Four at the beginning of the Daytona?"

Tracey was silent for a few moments. "Well, I'd probably be doing about one-sixty around the low part of the corner, then I'd back off a little and take it—"

"Wait a minute, your tires are still going to be cold," Rick reminded her.

She shook her head. "I'd have built up some tire pressure on the first straightaway. Then my speed could hit maybe one-eighty on the back straightaway before Turn Four."

"Don't forget the banking in Turn Three. That would slow you down."

Her eyes clouded a little. "You're right. I'd have to go into that turn low and set up my apex through the turn."

"But the pressure in your tires would be higher—so you could afford to kick up the speed a little."

"I know, but—"

"And don't forget all the plotting and jockeying going on with the other drivers."

"I'll be doing plenty of jockeying myself, don't forget." Tracey tried to sound confident. After all, her father had taught her everything she needed to know about the Daytona 500. She had the track practically memorized. "I can handle it."

"It means always expecting the unexpected."

"Is this part of my driver's training class? Will I have an exam at the end of the day?" She tried to mask her uncertainty in sarcasm.

"Probably. Multiple choice and then short essay." He offered her a sudden, arresting smile.

"There speaks the son of an English teacher," she countered. Her doubts about her driving dissolved as she fell in with Rick's lighthearted mood.

"No need to be insulting—" Rick continued playfully. But he halted abruptly as a shotgun-like sound sliced through the air.

"Oh, no!" Tracey exclaimed as she gripped the wheel to keep the car steady. "The left rear tire blew." She steered the car on a straight line, slowly moving it to the right until she felt the soft gravel on the side of the highway.

"I'll take care of it," Rick said as he started to scramble out of the car.

"Wait a minute. I'm driving. I think I should fix the flat," Tracey protested. She didn't want to play the helpless female.

"Look, we can't waste any time. Let me do it,"

Rick's voice was smooth but insistent. He didn't want her to feel like he was making her prove herself all the time.

Tracey kept her hands on the steering wheel, staring straight ahead. "Rick, I can do it."

"Tracey, I can do it."

"It's my car."

"Okay, let's both change it," Rick proposed. "You put the jack in place. I'll crank it up. And then you put the tire on."

Tracey nodded with a taut jerk of her head. She slipped out of the car, careful of the vehicles speeding past them, and walked around to the trunk. Once she found the jack, she went over to the flat tire and felt under the rim of the chassis for the best place to angle the jack. "Okay, it's all yours, Rick," she said as she inserted the handle into place.

"Not bad. One would think you'd done this before," Rick joked as he started to crank the handle.

Tracey watched the back of the car start to lift off the ground, mentally ticking off the minutes they were losing in the rally. She tapped her foot impatiently. But as she watched Rick's muscular arms pumping the jack, her thoughts started to drift away from the rally. His arm muscles were rippling in the most fascinating way and a wayward strand of dark hair tumbled over his forehead.

"Ready for the tire," Rick said as he locked the handle into place.

"Just . . . just a minute," Tracey responded dazedly as she went back to the trunk for the spare. Get a grip,

she told herself. The guy is changing a tire, for goodness sake. I can't go soft in the knees just because he's
handy during an emergency.

"Here it is." Tracey rolled the tire over and set it
into the rear axle. Then she picked up the lug wrench
to tighten the nuts.

Rick watched Tracey's slim, capable hands move
with efficient speed. How could she change a tire and
still look so delightfully feminine? And her hair seemed
to be lit with a thousand red-gold flames under the hot
Florida sun.

"How much time do you think we've lost?" Tracey
asked as she tightened the last bolt.

"Time. Right. Uh . . . let's see," Rick looked down
at his watch, trying to focus his eyes on the numbers
on the dial. How could he concentrate on time? *The
rally. Keep in mind we're here to win the rally.*
"Maybe ten minutes."

"What!" Tracey quickly jerked the jack handle back
and forth to let the car back down. "Let's get moving!"

Once they were back in the car speeding down the
highway, Tracey took a deep breath and tried to relax.

"We've still got a chance to hold onto our lead,"
Rick reassured her.

She looked at him quickly, hopefully. "You think
so?"

"I know so. Relax. Don't think about winning—
just drive."

She nodded, her eyes focused on the road. "Okay.
You're the expert."

The amusement died from his eyes and he regarded

her with searching gravity. Expert. Was that how she saw him? As a racer she could learn from and nothing more? Wasn't there something else going on between them? Rick's jaw tightened as he turned to look out the window at the scenery rolling past them. He may feel his heart skyrocket every time he saw her, but that didn't mean she felt the same way.

He had come to Daytona to finish the race—to win on the track that had haunted him for so long. That race meant everything to him. He'd given up a lucrative engineering job, invested his own money—all to get back into racing. Maybe he was destined to drift for the rest of his life and never find that anchor he was looking for.

Tracey was a complication he hadn't foreseen. He'd had relationships before, but they were always light-hearted and uncomplicated. Women who wanted to be seen with a race car driver and who liked to be photographed at the races. Tracey was nothing like those women. She challenged him, competed with him, and yet somehow stirred tender feelings in him that he'd never known he was capable of feeling. *What's happening to me? It's almost as if I'm in love. And I can't be. I've got a race to win.*

Tracey stole a quick glance at Rick and the absorbed look on his face told her the whole story. He was regretting teaming up with her in the rally. An experienced driver would have been able to change the tire faster—or at least not argued about who would change the tire.

Being a rookie was only part of the problem. She

was starting to feel like she could rely on him, confide in him. This was only their second day in the car together, but glancing over at his sharp, confident profile was becoming a familiar pleasure.

The isolated cocoon of the car separated them from the rest of the world and she was beginning to like that feeling, so much so she feared she might forget about the ultimate destination of the rally. For goodness sake! She'd only been in his company for twenty-four hours. How would she feel by the end of the rally?

Tracey clamped her jaw tight and stared at the road ahead of her. She'd chosen her way after Roger—and that path didn't include Rick. Besides, he didn't need a rookie slowing him down. He wanted to win as much as she did.

By the time they'd reached the check-in point at St. Petersburg, Tracey could feel her head throbbing. She didn't know if it was anxiety over the lost time or the tension of trying to ignore what was happening between her and Rick.

"Are we the first?" Tracey asked the check-in official.

"Nope. Another car came in five minutes ago." He pulled out his check list. "Danvers team, right?"

"You got it," Tracey beamed. They were only five minutes behind the lead driver. Hooray! They could make that up in the next three hours it took to get to Sanibel Island.

"I told you to relax," Rick reminded Tracey as she sped away from the check-in point. "A few lost minutes doesn't mean the whole race is shot."

Tracey gave him a sheepish grin. "I know. I over-reacted. It's just that this is my first rally and I—"

"Want to win?"

"You know I do."

"We've got a fighting chance to do it, even if we're second today," Rick reflected. "Our points from yesterday were high enough that we could afford to lose a few today."

Tracey's chin raised in determination. "I haven't given up on regaining those five minutes."

"Just don't speed, Miss Danvers." A wry but indulgent glint appeared in his eyes. "I'd hate to get a ticket for the first time in my life."

"Not to worry," Tracey declared loftily. "I'm in perfect control—"

"Tracey pull over," Rick's voice was suddenly hard and flat.

"What?"

"I said, pull over—the engine's overheating." Rick motioned with his arm. Once Tracey had stopped the car on the side of the road, Rick pointed at the temperature gauge. "Haven't you been checking the gauges?"

"Of course. It must've just shot up in the last ten minutes." A tiny furrow appeared between her brows as she frowned in concentration. It was hot today, but not the kind of heat that caused engines to overheat so quickly. "There could be a leak in radiator—"

Rick nodded. "That's what I think. We'll have to let it cool down for a few minutes." He reached back and pulled a gallon jug of distilled water out of the back seat. ''Let's check the engine.''

Rick felt the hood of the car. ''It's warm, but I think we can open it.''

Tracey held her breath as he slowly opened the hood. Only a little steam filtered out. ''Looks like we're okay,'' Tracey said thankfully.

Rick unscrewed the radiator cap and peered inside. ''Hmm. Just as I thought. It's almost empty. We've got a leak somewhere.''

''Oh, no,'' Tracey moaned. ''There's no way we'll be able to fix it out here.''

Rick studied the engine thoughtfully. ''We'll have to let it cool down. Then fill the radiator and try to make it to Sanibel as best we can.''

''I checked the radiator this morning. I couldn't have missed anything,'' Tracey muttered to herself as she crossed her arms in a defensive posture.

''It's not your fault. It could've been a hairline crack that got bigger. I'll get Skid and the guys down to Sanibel tonight—''

A horn honking made them both turn around. It was Paco. He waved to them with a casual flick of his fingers, and then sped by.

Rick stared after the car and then shrugged. ''Win some, lose some.''

Tracey whirled around and demanded. ''What do you mean by that?''

''Just what I said—''

''I didn't enter this rally to lose.''

A shadow of annoyance crossed his face. "Being prepared to lose is as important as wanting to win."

"So you're saying I should be a loser like Paco?" Tracey could feel her frustration pushing her to the edge.

"Of course not. I mean—"

"Drive to lose? Is that what you mean?"

"No!" Rick's patience snapped. "Why do you think Paco sat there last night, bending our ears with his pathetic stories?"

"I don't know—"

"To get your sympathy so you couldn't pass him by and win. But *he* did it today—and it made you mad because you thought you were friends."

"But—"

"Listen, Tracey," he grasped her arms. "Yesterday was great. No problems. We sailed along. But today, we've had the tables turned. Flat tire. Engine over-heats—all unexpected. But's that how you learn."

"I know how to deal with emergencies." Her tone was mutinous.

Rick shook his head. "I'm not talking about fixing a tire or cooling down an engine—those are details. I'm talking about the mental games. Your focus. Because what you're thinking and doing are going to have an impact on your driving."

Tracey stared wordlessly at him, her heart pounding. "What are you saying?"

"This is just a rally and you think you've failed because of an overheated engine, when it's really just an unforeseen occurrence." His face was only inches from hers, his grey eyes somehow intense and gentle at the same time. ''You accept it and go on because things don't always work out the way we plan them. That's it. No promises.''

Under his steady scrutiny, Tracey felt her anger drain away. He wasn't just talking about the rally, but something deeper—something she wasn't prepared to accept. ''Can I at least be disappointed?'' she asked with a tiny smile.

Rick squeezed her arms lightly. ''Any time. That's expected. It's just not the end. There's always another race.''

''I'm sorry, Rick.'' Tracey's eyes traveled over his face to the scar. ''Is this part of my training?''

''Let's just call it advice,'' Rick answered almost sadly. He'd learned those lessons the hard way and he'd do anything he could to keep Tracey from suffering the same mistakes he had. They'd made him foolhardy. And he'd paid bigtime.

''I guess the engine's cooled off by now,'' Tracey said quietly.

Rick's hands dropped to his side. Time to move on. ''You're right. I'll fill the radiator and we can be on our way.''

Tracey felt like cold water had been poured on her as she watched Rick fill the radiator. She could've kicked herself for being so stupid. She'd been so quick to jump on him, accuse him, when he was only giving her the benefit of his experience and judgment. Suddenly, she had this absurd desire to burst into tears, and her eyes started to blur. She blinked back the tears rapidly. There wasn't time for that, she reminded herself sternly. They had to get moving. If they lost any more time, they wouldn't stand a chance of holding on to their lead.

As Rick finished filling the radiator, he hoped Tracey hadn't noticed the tremor in his hands as he held the water jug. He hadn't felt a surge of emotion like that since before his crash and it almost overwhelmed him. He'd kept such a tight rein on his emotions, pretending nothing much mattered—except getting to run the Daytona 500 again. But he was only lying to himself. Something else did matter, maybe more that anything, and that was Tracey Danvers. He was almost numbed by the realization. *Get a grip, man.* He had to keep his thoughts straight or he'd be no use to her as part of her team.

"Okay. Ready to roll," Rick said as he lowered the hood. He had to keep focused. "Let's make up that time."

"You said it, partner," Tracey said as she slid behind the wheel, her spirits recovering once more. "Sanibel—here we come."

Unfortunately, Tracey's good humor didn't last long.

The next three hours proved to be the most nerve-wracking she had ever spent behind the wheel. The radiator leak kept getting larger and, while Rick tried to tape it, it still kept draining and was almost empty every half hour. Tracey would then have to pull over before the engine started to overheat, and Rick would refill the radiator.

After the fifth time they had to pull over, Tracey was in a cold sweat. Rick's features looked strained and she caught him running his hand through his hair in frustration. They stopped talking—not in anger— but so they could concentrate on keeping track of the temperature gauge. Eventually, the car limped onto Sanibel Island and to the South Beach Hotel where the rally drivers were staying.

Once they arrived, Tracey wearily hauled herself out of the car and walked into the hotel without a backward glance at Rick. She didn't have the energy to speak at this point.

When she reached her room, she collapsed on the bed. How could anything have been more horrible than the day they had today? Their car had broken down, they'd screamed at each other on the side of the road, they'd had to pull over almost every twenty minutes on the way to Sanibel. . . . Tracey couldn't remember when she'd had a more awful day. What a difference from their arrival yesterday with the pictures and Rick's proud assertion that they were a team. He probably wouldn't even want to finish the rally with her after today.

Chocolate. I need chocolate. First I need a shower, then I'm going to scour this hotel for a chocolate-covered almond.

Once Tracey had taken a shower, she felt the weight of the day's defeat start to lessen. *What had Rick said? I've got to be willing to lose before I win? Well, I've had my share of loss today.*

As Tracey started to unzip her travel case, she noticed the hotel staff had placed a single pink rose in a vase on her dresser. A note was attached that said: ''Let's celebrate our win today. Please join me in Room 212, Rick.''

Tracey re-read the card several times. A small smile of enchantment touched her lips. Rick knew just how to lift her spirits. But what did he have in mind by asking her to come to his room? Her thoughts drifted to images of tuxedoed waiters serving them exotic food, romantic violins playing tender music in the background, and Rick's handsome face whispering sweet nothings. A tremor ran through her. They had seen each other at their worst today—now they could see the best.

Tracey quickly donned the softly flowing gauzy dress of the night before and left her hair falling free on her shoulders. She picked up the rose at the last minute and inhaled its sweet scent. It was the essence of romance itself. Was that why Rick had sent it to her?

Minutes later Tracey rapped a nervous hand on Rick's hotel door. When he answered he was wearing a casual white cotton V-neck sweater and grey pants. Her heart thumped at the sight of him, standing there so tall and wide-shouldered.

''I got your message,'' she said as she held out the rose.

''Somehow I thought pink would suit you more than red,'' Rick commented as he motioned her into the room. ''Red might clash with your hair.''

Tracey bent her head. "First, I want to apologize for—"

"There's nothing to apologize about. We had a bad day, that's all."

"But—"

"Forget it."

She gave a forced smile and a tense nod of consent. "Okay. I guess it *was* a learning experience after all. . . ."

Rick's lips started to twitch. Tracey felt her own mouth curving into a smile, and soon she was shaking. Rick's laughter was a full-hearted sound that warmed her. Tracey's hands crept up to his shoulders as she hung on him for support.

"Can you believe those last three hours?" Tracey finally got out, still chuckling.

"Pure hell," Rick answered. There was still a trace of laughter in his voice.

"I don't know how we made it."

"Your expert driving, of course. You knew just how far to push the car." Rick suddenly noticed how close they were standing.

Tracey's cheeks turned almost as pink as the rose at the compliment. She realized then that she was practically leaning against Rick. Hastily, she drew her hands away and placed some distance between Rick and her. "So, what did you have in mind for tonight?" Tracey tried to sound nonchalant, but she was scanning the room for any sign of a romantic dinner.

"I've got a surprise for you. Remember the extra duffle I brought along?"

Tracey nodded, feeling puzzled. What could be in that duffle bag?

"Just wait—" He was interrupted by a knock at the door. "That'll be room service."

As Rick went to answer the door, Tracey's eyes brightened in anticipation. A table had been set up in front of the window overlooking the Gulf of Mexico. Tracey stood by the window and watched the gentle waves rolling in. Nothing could be more romantic. Rick must have ordered a special dinner. It would just be the two of them. Finally. Their romantic dinner.

"I hope you don't mind—I ordered some sandwiches and drinks for us while we watch the films," Rick said as he brought a tray heaped with assorted sandwiches into the room. He set them down on the table.

Tracey's brows knit in bafflement. What was going on? "What films?" she asked.

Rick pulled several videos out of the duffle bag. "I had some racing footage dubbed to videotape. I thought we could watch some this evening."

As Rick slipped a video into the VCR, Tracey was too startled to offer any objection. Finally, she cleared her throat. "Rick, where did you get the idea to bring racing videos?"

Rick had his back to her, since he was adjusting the picture on the television screen. "Your brother—Troy. He said you loved watching racing films. So I brought some along."

I will kill that twin of mine yet, Tracey fumed to herself.

Rick turned at her silence. "Is that okay?"

She managed a thin smile. "Sure—I can't think of anything else I'd like to do more." She picked up a half of a chicken salad sandwich and bit into it despondently.

Rick took a deep breath, his back still to Tracey. He didn't want her to see the deep disappointment in his face. He'd brought the videos at Troy's prompting but, secretly, he wanted to do anything *but* view some stupid videos. He wanted to watch the magnificent sunset over the still Gulf waters with Tracey's head resting against her shoulder. See her hair in the moonlight. . . . But Tracey only had one thought in mind— racing.

As Rick started the video, he sat down next to Tracey and helped himself to a sandwich. *Oh, well, this is better than nothing. At least we're together.*

"This was my race at Darlington last September," Rick said as he pointed at the screen.

Tracey squinted her eyes. "Let me turn out the lights—I can't make out the cars too well."

"I'll get them." He switched off the lights and then seated himself again. "The quality isn't too good—I had the film dubbed the day before we left on the rally."

"That's better," Tracey said absently. She was watching the green car nudging close to Rick's. "Is that Fielding in the green car?"

"Yeah." Rick's voice was grim in the darkness. "He plays it pretty close to the edge."

"You're telling me. He's only about two inches from you."

"He's the one you've got to keep your eye on at the beginning of the Daytona," Rick advised. "He takes a lot of chances to jockey for position—and doesn't care who he bangs up in the process."

"Haven't the NASCAR officials warned him?"

Rick nodded. "He's even been fined. The other drivers are going to have to put pressure on him."

"How?"

"Nudge him a little, crowd him in—nothing bad, but enough to get the message across that we're not going to risk our lives because he can't draw the line between risk and foolhardiness."

Tracey's breathing grew more rapid as her eyes followed Rick's Grand Prix around the track. "How hard is Darlington?"

"About the same as Daytona—but maybe a little easier than Bristol," Rick said. "Bristol's so short and the corners are banked so high, you're driving with your neck locked most of the time."

Tracey turned her head to look at Rick. He was engrossed in the race, driving each turn in his mind, feeling the wheel in his strong hands. The light from the television screen flickered across his face, illuminating his scar.

Sensing her scrutiny, Rick's eyes captured hers. "Were you wondering about this?" His hand traced the scar.

"No, no," Tracey answered hastily.

"It's okay." Rick gave her a lopsided smile. "I accepted it a long time ago."

"Was it the crash at Daytona?" Tracey asked, her voice soft.

"I was thrown from the car and my helmet cracked apart. They told me that a piece of metal must have sliced across my face," he said matter-of-factly. "I was thankful that I didn't lose my eye."

"Is that . . . why you stopped racing? The crash?" Tracey asked before she could stop herself. She had wanted to ask him yesterday, but the time never seemed right.

Rick was silent for a few moments. "You mean, did I lose my nerve? Maybe. I don't know. I only know I lost my desire to race. I couldn't face risking my life, drifting, and having no one at the end of the race." Rick looked back at the screen, watching himself in the speeding car. "I wanted to play it safe, I guess, and that's why I went into engine design. But after a while, I got restless for driving again.

"But I realized today how much of myself I had shut down since the crash. I don't think I've really felt anything inside for a long time. Maybe I still have to prove to myself that I have the nerve . . . ," his voice trailed off.

"To win?" Tracey asked, searching his features.

Rick gave a short laugh. "Maybe. I won't really know till I'm in the car at the Daytona."

"But you've had a winning streak at some of the other races," Tracey pointed out. She wanted to reach out and touch his face, hold him tightly in her arms.

"They're not the Daytona."

"I know."

Silence filled the room.

"Maybe this wasn't such a good idea," Rick finally said in a clipped voice. He jerked to his feet and snapped the television off. The room was plunged into darkness. Just at that moment, Tracey stood up. She tried to make out his features, but they were just a shadow.

"Rick . . . I . . . ," Tracey faltered as she felt Rick's hands threading through her hair.

"We've got to be sensible," Rick reminded her in a low, husky whisper. His fingers moved to the back of her neck and down her shoulders. He wanted to feel the softness of her skin.

"You're right," Tracey answered as she moved closer into the circle of his arms. "We've got a race to win."

"Who cares about winning?" Rick said as he hugged her tightly.

Chapter Eight

Tracey put her arms around his neck. Very softly she kissed him. It was a sweet, gentle kiss that stirred him to his very soul. It told him that she understood his vulnerability and didn't think he was any less of a man for it.

"I guess that's what it means to have a partner—someone to talk to," Tracey whispered, her head against his shoulder.

"And someone to listen." Rick brushed a light kiss across her temple. The nearness of her made him shiver.

Tracey's body seemed oddly weightless. She felt she wanted to spend the rest of her life in Rick's arms. That was where she belonged—she knew that. Suddenly, winning didn't seem all that important. Was that what Rick was trying to tell her?

"Rick, I—"

"Rick! Rick! Are you in there?" Someone was hammering at the door.

"What's Skid doing here already?" Rick exclaimed.

"Skid?"

"The pace car—you know—the one that kept breaking down on us today?" Rick reminded her gently. "I

138

called Skid to come down with one of my mechanics to fix it. But I didn't think they'd get here so soon.''

Tracey was reluctant to leave Rick's arms and he didn't seem in any hurry to let her go. ''We could ignore him—and maybe he'll just leave,'' she said as she ran her fingers across his strong jaw, feeling the slight stubble. He captured her hand and kissed it tenderly.

Rick groaned and gently disentangled his arms from around Tracey. ''You don't know Skid.'' He switched the lights back on.

''Bad timing,'' Tracey said as she smoothed down her hair.

Rick gave her a sidelong glance. ''I'll say.''

''Rick!'' Skid's voice boomed on the other side of the door.

Rick shrugged in mock resignation. As he slowly opened the door, Skid burst in.

''Okay, Rick, what gives?'' Skid tossed off as he threw his tool bag on the floor. ''You call with an emergency, then I can't find you. When I do get your room number, I've got to beat on the door like a maniac. What are you—'' He broke off as he caught sight of Tracey. ''What's she doing here?''

''My rally partner, remember?'' Rick answered with some asperity in his voice.

''Oh, right.'' The room fell silent. Skid eyed Tracey and then Rick. ''Did I . . . interrupt something?''

''We were trying to figure out our strategy for tomorrow,'' Tracey answered a bit too hastily. ''To regain our lead.''

"Uh-huh," Skid responded. Silence again.

"Tracey had some good suggestions," Rick added
with a half-hearted attempt at a smile.

"I'll bet."

Tracey stirred uneasily in her chair.

"Okay . . . well . . . let's talk about fixing that
cracked radiator," Tracey prompted in a crisp voice.
Why did she feel so awkward? They had nothing to
hide from Skid. Or did they?

"Don't worry your pretty little head about it," Skid
agreed. "Rick and I can take care of it."

Tracey bristled at the implication. "What is that
supposed to mean? I've worked on engines all my life,
Mr. Parker."

"I'm sure." Skid winked at Rick, a gesture that did
not go unnoticed by Tracey.

"I don't like your patronizing tone—"

"Skid was just having a little joke," Rick inter-
vened. Why did Skid always say the exact wrong thing
to antagonize her? "But since you drove today, why
don't you get some rest while Skid and I work on the
car?"

"All right," Tracey said in a slightly mollified tone,
though her eyes narrowed as she shot a look back at
Skid. Macho type.

"Tomorrow will be *our* day," Rick said softly as
he led Tracey to the door.

A new and unexpected warmth shot through Tracey
at his words. Just the thought of them in the car together
tomorrow made her feel absurdly happy. One more day

of Rick and her being partners. She would savor every moment of it. It would be a memory she could take with her.

"Tomorrow, then."

As Rick closed the door and turned back into the room, he frowned at his crew chief. Skid's mouth was twisted in a decidedly sarcastic way.

"What's wrong?" Rick exclaimed, a note of impatience in his voice.

"You're asking me?" Skid queried back.

Rick nodded with a taut jerk of his head. "Yes, I am."

"Okay, cards on the table, man," Skid had an edge to his voice. "You're getting caught up with that Danvers girl and it's going to cost you. And if it costs you, it's going to cost me. Face it. She's trouble. Maybe she's even stringing you along to get you so crazy you can't even think straight when you've got to race against her."

"Skid—" Rick's voice held a warning note.

"Look, I'm not trying to tell you how to live. But this is a dangerous thing to do. You've got to see that."

"I can handle it."

"Can she?" Skid challenged. "If you care about her, you'll stop it right now."

Rick felt a distinct chill at his crew chief's warning. Was Skid right? Was he being selfish reaching out to the one woman who made him feel alive again? Tracey had become too important to him to let her ruin her chances at achieving her dream. "Don't sweat it, Skid.

I know what I'm doing,'' Rick said with a quiet assurance he was far from feeling.

''I hope so.''

''The car seems to be running tiptop,'' Tracey commented as they sped through the Everglades, on the last leg of the rally.

Rick nodded. ''It didn't take long to fix it last night. Skid brought a spare radiator and we replaced the cracked one. Simple, really.''

Tracey studied Rick's set features in puzzlement. What happened to him? Where was the man who held her in his arms and kissed her like he'd never let her go? He seemed as remote as a granite statue this morning. ''So what are our chances of regaining our lead?''

''Fair,'' he gauged. ''If our luck holds out and we don't have any breakdowns, maybe even better.''

My luck has apparently run out, Tracey thought miserably to herself. Rick must've had second thoughts last night about their relationship. The glowing admiration she'd seen in his eyes last night was replaced by a distant preoccupation. Maybe he was embarrassed by what he'd revealed to her last night. He'd shown her part of the inner Rick and maybe he was having second thoughts about their ''partnership.'' Obviously, his whole demeanour had changed. *I just can't seem to get the signals right.*

''Looks a little eerie, doesn't it?'' Rick broke into her thoughts.

''What?''

"The Everglades—" Rick gestured out toward the grassy swampland all around them.

Tracey hadn't even noticed how the morning sun filtered strange purple lights through the tall, waving grasses. And how the cabbage palms cast weird shadows almost like they had tentacle-like arms reaching down into the shallow water. "I expect to see some type of swamp creature coming out of there at any moment," Tracey commented.

Rick chuckled lightly. "Small chance. But you might see an alligator."

"I wouldn't tangle with one of them this time of year—mating season's coming up and they get very testy."

"That'll do it," Rick said with a flicker of amusement in his eyes. "Speaking of which—"

"Yes?" Tracey heart thumped in anticipation.

Rick took in a deep breath and then he took the plunge. "I want to apologize for last night. We agreed to be partners for the rally—partners, not soulmates. I guess I was wired from everything that happened yesterday and I lost my head. I didn't have any right to lay my emotional baggage on you." He felt like he was picking his way through a mine field. After Skid's warning, Rick had kicked himself mentally through most of the night for letting his emotions get carried away.

"Rick, it's okay—"

His hands flexed on the steering wheel in frustration. "Look, you're not my confessor. Every answer I need to find is going to be on that race track at Daytona. I don't have any right to embroil you in my problems.''

''But what about my feelings?'' Tracey protested, hope kindling in her breast at Rick's words. He confided in her—he must care about her.

''That's what I'm trying to consider—your feelings. We've been in this car together alone for three days and that can do strange things to your head. You're . . . you're like no other woman I've ever met—so beautiful, so full of life—you make me feel like it's possible to have all the things I've lost since the accident.'' Rick felt the words coming slowly, haltingly. ''But we need to remember why we entered this rally in the first place—and not let anything else get in the way.''

''I see,'' Tracey said woodenly, feeling a tiny stab of disappointment in her heart. What had she expected? Rick still had to prove himself and, until then, he wasn't ready to let her come between him and racing.

''I don't think you do. It's because of you, Tracey,'' Rick said with quiet emphasis. ''I'm also thinking about what you want.''

''I want . . . ,'' she trailed off as she bowed her head. What could she say? That she wanted to share everything with him? His life and his pain? She wasn't sure. She still had her own dream. Suddenly her eyes fastened on the open map. ''I want . . . to take the Miami by-pass. It'll cut at least thirty minutes off of our time.''

''What?'' Rick's eyes blinked in astonishment.

''The by-pass,'' Tracey urged, pointing at the intersecting road. ''Make a right here. Now!''

Rick signaled and jerked the wheel to the right. The car abruptly swung around throwing Tracey against him. Her body made contact with his and then was thrown back against the door as Rick straightened the car out.

"Give me a little more notice next time." His mouth twisted wryly.

"Sorry."

"No problem." Rick stared ahead at the miles of flat road. Straight and flat. That was the road ahead of him. He had his answer. Tracey was on her own road and that didn't include him. He had to accept that—for her sake.

"I think we're ahead of the pack again," she said shakily as she smoothed her hair back into the headband that held it off her face.

"That's the important thing, isn't it?" Rick asked in a quiet voice.

Tracey nodded, her face turned toward the window, so Rick couldn't see the shimmer of tears in her eyes. Her feelings for Rick went deeper than anything she'd ever known—but how could she tell him that? But there was no room for her in his life. He had races to win. . . .

"Looks like we got our luck back today," Rick tried to interject a light note into the leaden silence of the car.

"Looks like it," Tracey agreed. But she'd never felt more unlucky in her entire life.

By the time they reached the overseas bridges that link the Keys, Tracey and Rick both knew they had outdistanced everyone else on the rally. The by-pass had helped them regain lost time.

"Do you think we made enough points today to make up for yesterday?" Tracey inquired as her glance drifted out over the shimmering water that surrounded them on both sides.

"Maybe. We've got a good chance. And I haven't seen Paco since we started this morning."

"True."

"*His* luck hasn't changed."

Serves him right, Tracey thought. She tried not to feel vindicated. But Paco had acted like a jerk. He not only had zipped past them yesterday when they had car problems, he gloried in their troubles.

"Key West is probably going to be crowded when we get to the finish line," she speculated. The image of cheering crowds suddenly depressed her because it signaled the end of the rally—and the end of the time she shared with Rick.

"I guess so."

Tracey took a deep breath. "Since we won't have much time to talk afterwards, I want to tell you . . . to say how much I appreciate your driving with me. I know I'm still a rookie and everything—and I did panic yesterday. I know it. But I also learned something."

Rick's brows rose expectantly.

"I learned. . . . " How she longed to reach out and touch his face, lean her head against his shoulder. "I learned . . . how to do a two-man tire change."

Rick gave a short bark of laughter. "You mean one-man, one-woman tire change team."

Tracey's lips widened in a bittersweet smile. "We really have been a team, haven't we?"

"Absolutely. I can't think of any other person I'd want by my side—"

"Tracey—"

"Rick!" Tracey almost shouted in excitement. "We're here. We've made it!" She gestured at the "Finish" sign ahead of them.

Rick grasped her hand tightly as he steered the car past the finish line. Hundreds of people had gathered, all screaming and throwing confetti. They surrounded the car as Rick finally brought it to a halt. He took one last look at Tracey, her face animated and alive, and he realized he had never before felt so defeated.

"Good luck, Tracey," he said as he gave her hand a tiny squeeze.

"Wait," Tracey protested as he started to get out of the car. But, at that instant, James Danvers opened her car door.

"Tracey! Great job!" he shouted over the crowd. He helped her out and hugged her tightly. "You did it!"

"Are we first?" Tracey almost screamed.

"You sure are. Paco Carrera dropped out two hours ago. Engine trouble again. He was your only competition."

"Rick! Did you hear that?" She turned to find Rick, but Skid was already drawing him away from the car. Her lips tightened for a moment.

Her father put an arm around her as they started to thread through the crowd. "What's wrong?"

"Nothing." She flashed him an overly bright smile. "I only wish Troy were here."

James rolled his eyes. "He wanted to . . . but I made him stay off that foot. He's been impossible. Mrs. Carleton has had to practically tie him to the bed."

Tracey smiled, knowing her twin's impatience with any physical impediment.

"More good news—your engine timing is stable. Jake and I were able to fix the restrictor plates and the engine is practically purring."

Tracey patted her father absently. "That's great, Dad." But her eyes were still sweeping the crowd for Rick.

"Time for the winner's circle—your first, but not your last," James said proudly.

As they approached the winner's circle, Tracey saw Rick. His back was to her and he was deep in conversation with Skid.

"Dad, I want to get Rick so we can have a picture together," Tracey explained.

James nodded. "I'll tell the photographers."

As Tracey approached the two men, she heard Skid's voice exclaiming with admiration, "I've got to hand it to you, Rick. You're a genius. You and that rookie female—"

"Skid." Rick looked impatient. "She has a name."

"Yeah, right. Oh, man, what a publicity stunt! I can see the headlines now: 'MASTERS SHARES WIN WITH PRETTY ROOKIE.' When the sponsors see that, you can name your own price! You were way ahead of me, man. Think of the promotions—"

"Set up a meeting with the sponsors tonight, Skid, following the press conference."

Tracey was stunned. Surely Rick hadn't been thinking only of publicity? How could he use her like this? Was everything between them a lie. Just like Roger? She thought she had had problems picking up Rick's wavelength, but she couldn't have been that off frequency. Could she?

Skid said, "Why wait till tonight? The press is clamoring right now—"

"We need to talk first. But right now I want to find Tracey. She'll need help in dealing with—"

"I don't need your help," Tracey announced, trying to hide the hurt behind a firm voice and a set jaw. "I catch on fast."

Skid looked back and forth between them and then said: "Well, I've gotta make a few phone calls. . . . " He jogged off.

Rick's tone was irascibly patient as he took Tracey's arm to steer her through the crowd. "Don't mind Skid, Tracey. He's just excited about—"

Tracey tried to yank her arm away. "I know what he was excited about. The success of your big publicity stunt. Rick, how could you do this to me—to us?"

"Now wait a minute." Rick's fingers tightened around her arm, halting her. "You don't think I really did that just for the publicity, do you?"

"You tell me," she countered.

"Skid was jumping to conclusions."

"I didn't exactly hear you disagreeing—"

"I would have straightened him out," he interrupted

vehemently, "before he gave out any statements to the press."

Her stormy green eyes clashed with his cool greys. "Right. And you were going to coach me, too, on what to say. So I wouldn't interfere with your big headline."

"What can I say, Tracey?" he said with quiet anger. "You seem to have made up your mind."

"Picture time!" James appeared, followed by a troop of eager photographers.

"Rick, step into the winner's circle and move a little closer to Tracey." A short man with a large, complicated looking camera hanging around his neck, motioned them together.

Tracey tried to edge closer to Rick without actually touching him.

"Tracey, I don't understand what you're so steamed up about," Rick said between clenched teeth in a semblance of a smile.

"Rick, put your arm around Tracey," another photographer said as he fired off shot after shot with his camera.

Tracey smiled sweetly into the camera as she hissed at Rick: "I don't like being used."

"I wasn't using you," Rick protested under his breath.

Tracey turned her head and flashed him a look of disdain. "I think you'd do anything to win."

"Are you talking about me or yourself?" Rick retorted, his grey eyes darkened like angry thunderclouds.

"Great shot!" The short photographer exclaimed. "Keep looking at each other like that—hold each other a little closer."

Rick tightened his arms around Tracey and, in spite of her anger, she had to fight not to lean into the hardness of his chest. Part of her wanted to dissolve into that weightless state she felt when she was in his arms. The crowd of people around them, the photographers snapping pictures melted away; and it was just the two of them—holding each other.

"I think that's enough," Tracey declared as she pushed out of Rick's arms. She was furious with him and even more furious with herself—how could she be angry and still react to his touch that way?

"Thanks, guys," Rick said to the photographers with an easy smile. "See you at the Daytona."

"In Victory Lane, Rick?" one of the photographers asked jokingly.

"Hard to say. With competition like this. . . . " He gestured toward Tracey. "Never can tell."

Tracey listened with a cynical smile. Rick certainly knew how to play the press to his advantage. He had the right balance between confidence and modesty— he gave away only what he had to. And they were eating out of his hand. But wasn't that one of the things he'd tried to tell her in the rally? Was he being upfront then and deceitful now? Or was everything a lie?

Once the photographers left, Rick turned back to Tracey and her father. "Are you staying for the festivities tonight? There's a barbecue and fireworks." Rick's eyes were on Tracey.

"Sure—" James Danvers started to answer.

"No, sorry," Tracey broke in. At her father's look of surprise, she continued hurriedly. "The Daytona is less than a week away—besides I don't want to leave Troy that long. He'll drive Mrs. Carleton crazy."

"True." James nodded thoughtfully. "Next time, Rick."

"Right, next time," Rick's eyes clung to hers, trying to pierce the distance between them. A heaviness centered in his chest. He couldn't leave her like this. He wanted to explain. "You were a great partner, Tracey."

"Anytime," she said brightly, feeling suspiciously close to tears.

"Are you—"

"Rick, got some guys over here who want to interview you." Skid tapped him lightly on the back.

Rick gave Tracey one last look, waiting for her to say something. She cast her eyes downward.

Skid gave a little shrug at the sudden silence. "Hey, sorry to break this up, but the reporters aren't going to wait all day."

"We'll take the pace car back, Rick," James offered. "See you in Daytona."

"Yeah...yeah, see you soon," Skid dismissed them as he drew Rick away. "Now, Rick, these guys want to ask some questions about your engine design and—"

Tracey watched them walk away with a suffocating sensation in her throat. People swirled around Rick, shaking his hand, slapping him on the back in congratulations, but he didn't look back at her. It seemed so final. Was Rick walking out of her life forever? She fought an urge to run after him, throw her arms around him and tell him—what? Suddenly, a thought froze in her brain. She loved him. There it was. Even if he had been using her for publicity in the rally, she now realized that she loved him anyway. She couldn't deny it any longer.

"Come on, Tracey, let's go home." James put an arm around her. "You won."

The word now had a bitter ring to her.

Chapter Nine

"**O**kay, Tracey, what gives?" Troy demanded as he hobbled into the kitchen early one morning.

Tracey gave him a blank stare.

"Don't give me that look," he warned in a disgusted voice. "I'm your twin, remember? I know when something's up with you. The Daytona 500 is tomorrow, you qualified in the top ten starting cars. You should be bouncing off the walls with excitement."

Tracey stirred her cereal desultorily. "I'm excited, Troy. I guess I'm a little worried, too—you know, this is the biggest race I've been in—"

"Sure, sure, and that's why you were so depressed about winning the rally, too," Troy cut in. He ran a critical eye over his sister's downcast features. Then he slid down into the chair next to her. His voice deepened with concern: "I'm only asking because I care about you. I've never seen you like this before."

I've never been in love before. Tracey managed a small, tentative smile. "Really, I'm just jittery before the race, that's all."

"Sure?"

"Sure."

Troy crossed his arms and leaned back in his chair. "I don't believe you."

"Don't you have anything better to do than badger your sister before the big race?" Mrs. Carleton asked with mock severity. Her large, fleshy arms carried a huge pile of laundry. "If you want to make yourself useful, why don't you strip the beds so I can wash the sheets?"

"Love to, Carley, but . . . uh . . . I've got to check Tracey's car over." Troy winked playfully at Tracey, and then scrambled out of his chair to make a quick exit.

"Nothing clears a man out of a room faster than asking him to help with laundry," Mrs. Carleton mused as she thumped the laundry basket on the table.

Tracey's gentle laughter rippled through the air. "You've got a point there."

Silence descended over the kitchen.

The older woman's big hands started folding towels with a dexterity born of long practice. "Your big day is finally here," she said as she concentrated on her task.

"It's hard to believe." Tracey tried to rouse a semblance of enthusiasm in her voice.

"All those years of practise and preparation—and it's going to happen tomorrow." Mrs. Carleton tilted her head to watch Tracey. "Not many people get the chance to have their dreams come true."

"I know—it's more than I'd hoped for." Tracey bent her head and studied her hands. "Dad always said

I had the hands of a driver—I guess I'll find out tomorrow if he was right.''

''The important thing is you have the chance—provided that's still what you want.''

''Of course it is,'' she answered sharply.

The older woman folded the last towel and then stacked them back in the laundry basket. ''Sometimes dreams change.''

''Mine don't,'' Tracey muttered.

Mrs. Carleton snorted. ''And sometimes you grow up to find your own.''

''I don't know why everyone's giving me the third degree this morning,'' Tracey exclaimed in irritation as she jumped to her feet. ''Nothing's changed. I'm going to drive in that race tomorrow and I'm going to win it. Trust me, I'm going to do it.''

''Stubborn. Just like—''

''Who's stubborn?'' Troy asked as he reappeared. ''Not me?''

Mrs. Carleton pursed her lips. ''That's for sure. You're just plain lazy.''

''I love you, Carley,'' Troy grabbed her and kissed her on the cheek. ''You tell it like it is.''

Mrs. Carleton pretended to endure Troy's affection with a long suffering roll of her eyes, but Tracey saw the love in her eyes.

Troy threw a pair of white overalls on the table. ''Come on, Tracey. Suit up. We need to go to Jake's to check your car over one more time.''

Tracey picked up the overalls in relief. Mrs. Carleton was getting too close to what was really bothering her—

and she just didn't want to talk about it. "Good idea. Let's get going." Maybe checking over her Thunderbird would keep Rick's image from appearing in her mind every hour.

"Tracey," Mrs. Carleton stopped her as she started out the kitchen door. "Trust your feelings."

Tracey froze. She couldn't turn around. If she did, she'd probably burst into tears. She took a deep breath and followed her brother out.

"What was she talking about?" Troy asked as soon as they were out of earshot.

"Who knows?" Tracey muttered. "You know how sentimental she is."

Troy grinned in agreement. "Underneath that crusty exterior beats a heart as big as all get-out."

He handed her a helmet.

"Wait a minute," Tracey halted abruptly in front of Troy's motorcycle. "I'm not getting on that thing."

"What do you mean?" he asked in an injured voice. "You drive stock cars."

"That's different. I'm in a car, not a seat on two wheels."

"Trust me."

Tracey reluctantly jammed the helmet onto her head. "Just take it easy on the speed."

Tracey revved the engine of her silver Thunderbird. It sounded good. Not a trace of vibration in the restrictor plates. The car had performed perfectly during the 125-Mile Qualifying Race—and it seemed ready to go for the Daytona tomorrow.

So why don't I feel thrilled with this success?

She leaned her head against the roof of the car with a sigh. One answer: Rick Masters.

She'd overreacted in Key West. She knew that now. She hadn't given Rick a chance to explain. Maybe he had been using her, but hadn't she been using him a little, too? After all, she'd wanted to drive with him in the rally partly because he was such a famous stock car racer. The pain she'd felt when she overheard him talking with Skid was left over from her relationship with Roger. He had tried to exploit her, trade on the Danvers name, but that didn't make Rick the same, she finally realized.

But only then did she realize she loved him. That changed everything.

She still wanted to win the Daytona—too many people were counting on her, too many people had invested in her for her to let them down. Besides, she still wanted it; the Daytona was her dream. But new dreams were replacing the old ones.

She had grown up in a man's world, but now she wanted the things any woman would want. Sure, she still wanted to race, but she was also thinking of a house—her house—maybe some kids, with dark hair and dark eyes like Rick.

Her mouth twisted in self-mockery. With Rick as their father? He hasn't even said he loved me. And he won't. *Get a hold of your fantasies, Tracey.* She stood up, straightened her overalls, and took a deep breath. Time to get back to work.

"Troy, I'm going to check the oil pan," Tracey

shouted to her twin as she positioned herself on the rolling dolly and slid under the car.

Keep your mind on work. You've got a race to win tomorrow.

"Troy, will you hand me a socket wrench," she asked as she heard his footsteps approach.

"Can't find it," he mumbled.

She gave an exclamation of impatience as she slid the dolly out from under her car. "It's right—" She broke off as she realized she was staring into the grey eyes of Rick Masters.

Rick drank in her pale features as though a drowning man. Even with a streak of grease across her forehead, she was enchanting. Suddenly, a thought occurred to him. "That was you under the car that day in the garage."

Tracey flushed.

"I kicked you the first time we met." His smile was apologetic. "It seems so long ago."

He echoed her own thoughts. Just hearing his voice, she felt the barriers she'd tried to erect around her heart melt. Those featherlike lines were crinkling around his eyes in the most attractive way.

Tracey stood up abruptly and walked over to the multilevel tool box. "Not so long—I still remember what Skid said about women racing," she tossed off diffidently over her shoulder.

Rick gritted his teeth. *Skid has a lot to answer for.* "It's like I was trying to tell you in Key West—Skid doesn't speak for me," Rick protested.

Tracey continued sifting through the tools. "Yeah, well, it really doesn't matter,"

"It does to me."

Tracey whirled around, the socket wrench in her hand. "Rick, what are you doing here?"

I couldn't stay away. I think about you constantly during the day and I dream about you at night. "I hope you're not going to use that on me." He looked pointedly at the wrench in her hand.

"Of course not." A ghost of a smile found its way through her mask of uncertainty. "You still didn't answer my question."

"I . . . wanted to see you, to congratulate you on your qualifying times. I heard you were in the top ten."

She shrugged to hide her disappointment. What did she expect? A declaration of love? "Thanks. I heard you got the pole position, so you'll be in the front row tomorrow."

"Just got lucky."

"That old luck thing again," Tracey commented.

"Look, Tracey," Rick walked forward, stopping in front of her. "I didn't like leaving Key West with things the way they were between us. Skid gets carried away sometimes—but that doesn't mean I agree with him."

"I know," she admitted. "I got carried away myself in Key West. I lost my temper and I'm sorry."

Rick pushed a few stray tendrils away from her cheek. "Must be the red hair."

She nodded woodenly. "It really doesn't matter."

"It matters to me—"

"The rally was great, Rick," Tracey raised her chin with a cool stare. "But like you said, three days in a car can do strange things to your mind. We're on different roads now."

"That's it?" Rick inquired in a dangerously low voice.

"It has to be."

Rick's fingers clamped around her arms. "Tracey Danvers, you're a coward!" he lashed out.

"I am not," she sputtered, bristling with indignation. Then she took a deep breath and continued in a calm voice. "I was in a relationship before with a racer—it didn't work out. He was using me and, when I found out, he didn't even bother to deny it."

"That was him—not me."

"Maybe it was him or maybe it was the competition. I don't know."

"So you're not afraid to let anything or anyone else come into your life." Rick's breath came raggedly in impotent anger.

"Look who's talking. You're the one who said you couldn't let anything else get in the way of your winning," she challenged.

Rick inhaled sharply. "Maybe I was wrong."

"And maybe you were just being realistic."

"That's not realism, that's obsession."

"And I suppose you're any different?" Tracey felt her control snap. Not caring about who might hear her, she shouted: "All you can think about is finishing that race tomorrow—the race that ended your career eight years ago. You want to win just as much as I do—

maybe more. Remember what you said? Anything to win. Not Paco, not me, nothing will stand in your way.''

Their turbulent emotions swirled around them like a stormy sea. But Tracey was too preoccupied with her own pain to see the hurt in Rick's grey eyes.

''I want to win. I won't deny that. I never did,'' Rick grated out. ''But I'm not denying what's between us either.''

''There's nothing between us, Rick. A few days together can't change what we are.'' But Tracey's stomach knotted at her own words. The rally *had* changed her. No longer did her heart hum to the sound of an engine—the days and nights she filled with racing now seemed strangely empty. She needed more—she needed Rick.

Rick's gaze travelled over her face and searched her eyes. His anger fell away as he registered the troubled confusion in those cloudy, green pools. His own heart tightened in frustration. He wanted to crush her in his arms, hold her tightly against his chest until she admitted that she wanted him as much as he wanted her. But he couldn't—it would only make matters worse.

Rick dropped his arms. ''Okay. If that's the way you want it, Tracey.''

She nodded, not trusting herself to answer.

Neither spoke as the silence stretched like a tense band between them, ready to snap.

''Good luck tomorrow,'' Rick finally said in a resigned voice. ''And I mean it.''

''Me, too.''

He swung around and was gone.

Tracey stood motionless in the middle of the garage. The only man she'd ever loved had just walked out of her life and she just stood there. She wanted to run after him, yell her love for him at the top of her voice. But what did he want? He never said he loved her. Tracey ran her hand over her forehead as she tried to force her confused emotions into order. What could she do?

She looked at the wrench she still held in her hand. "Damn it," she exclaimed as she threw it across the room.

Just at that moment, Jake lumbered in. He ducked as he caught sight of the flying wrench. It landed with a dull thud against the garage wall. "Hey, you could hurt somebody with that."

"Oh, God, I'm sorry, Jake." She rushed over to check that he was all right. "Are you okay?"

His large face split into a wide grin. "Barely winged me."

She shook her head as though coming out of a daze. "I don't know what got into to me."

"Must be the race," Jake said quietly.

"I feel wound tighter than a clock," Tracey agreed as she bent down to retrieve the wrench. "But don't worry—I've got it under control."

"Do you?" Jake questioned.

Tracey straightened up. "Of course. You know I'll run the best race—"

"I don't mean the race," Jake cut her off with a

wave of his large hand. "You were pretty hard on Rick."

Her body stiffened. "We just had a disagreement, that's all, Jake."

"Hmm. Sounded more like a lovers' quarrel."

It was pointless to try to lie to Jake, Tracey admitted to herself. He could read her feelings sometimes better than her own twin. "It wouldn't work—I know that."

"Have you given it a chance? Have you given *him* a chance?" Jake asked.

"Jake, forget it—"

"Tracey, you're like my own daughter." His voice held a note of gruff affection. "So, I'm telling you— you're wrong about Rick Masters. I've known him a long time and he's one guy you can trust. He's got some ghosts in his head from his crash, but he wouldn't ever let you down. Period."

Stabbing doubts filtered through Tracey's mind. What had she done? Did Rick love her? "Jake, three weeks ago I knew exactly what I wanted. Now, my life has been turned completely upside down and I don't know what I want anymore. Racing has been my whole life. I can't just let all my dreams go, can I?" Her question was a plaintive call for help.

Jake's hand gripped her shoulder reassuringly. "When two people get together, they find a way. You don't think this garage is my whole life? It's what I do, that's all. I go home to my wife and kids at the end of the day."

Tracey smiled in spite of her confusion. Jake's wife

was a tiny, plump woman who had this giant bear of a man wrapped around her finger.

"Race stock cars if you want, but don't forget to have a life." Jake took the wrench out of her limp hand and threw it into the toolbox.

Tracey's eyes drifted over to the silver Thunderbird, sleek and fast. It was like an old friend to her. It responded to her every need—except this one.

Chapter Ten

The crowd pulsed with excitement, impatient for the Daytona 500 to begin. Loudspeakers blared out the starting lineup. People were shouting names of their favorite driver. Everyone was standing, waiting for the forty drivers to fire up their engines.

"You're going to have to watch it. You're hyped up and you tend to overrev when shifting gears—you could blow the whole engine," Troy warned as he handed Tracey her helmet.

Tracey's eyes scanned the other cars lined up in their positions. The drivers were standing next to their cars, getting last minute instructions from their crew chiefs. Fielding was in the car next to her—he was pacing back and forth, muttering to himself. Paco was in the second row—right behind Rick whose broad shoulders stood out in the white racing suit.

"Tracey, are you listening to me?" Troy asked impatiently.

"Of course," she responded absently. "I won't ride the clutch or overrev the engine." Her eyes strayed back to Rick. He hadn't even looked back at her to see if she was in starting position. After yesterday—

"Don't be worried if the car is running too tight at

166

first—it'll loosen up as the track starts to heat up,''
Troy reminded her as he put his headset on. ''Time to
go—let's have a mike check.''

Tracey pulled her helmet on and adjusted the microphone. ''Testing . . . can you hear me?''

''Loud and clear, Tracey,'' Troy answered. He
stepped forward and clasped her body tightly to his in
a bearhug. ''Let's win this thing. You can do it, Tracey. I'll be your ears and eyes in the pit, and Dad will
be troubleshooting the pit crew.''

Tracey hugged her twin. ''I'm counting on you.''

''You got it.'' He squeezed her once more. ''We're
a team.''

Tracey tried not to wince at that word as she started
to slide into her Thunderbird. Just as she got her legs
in, she caught sight of Rick watching her. They both
had their helmets on, so she couldn't see his eyes, but
he gave her a thumbs-up sign. Tracey smiled to herself,
not knowing why she suddenly felt more lighthearted.
She waved at Rick and then pulled her head and shoulders into the car.

Troy snapped the protective grid over the window
opening. ''Let the car settle in for the first few laps—
you've got 200 to make your play.''

''All right, already, Troy. Get to the pit,'' Tracey
said as she strapped herself into the car.

Rick slid into his Grand Prix.

''Watch turn four—you're still taking it too high. It
cost you time during the qualifying run,'' Skid reminded him.

''No problem.''

"And keep your mind on the race—not on that rookie female. She can take care of herself."

"I'm driving to win, Skid. That's the bottom line." Rick fastened his safety harness. Winning was one thing—that didn't mean he wasn't aware of Tracey only three rows behind him.

"This is what we've worked for, Rick. But take it easy. You've got some history with this race—that's going to be in your head," Skid cautioned. He snapped the protective grid on Rick's window opening and then tapped the car twice. "For luck. This car is going to win the Daytona 500."

Rick nodded. He could already feel the tension starting in the back of his neck. His fellow drivers weren't the real challenge to him today. It was all the old ghosts that threatened to spring out at him—especially turn four, where he had crashed eight years ago. Maybe that's why he always took it too high. He still imagined his car lying at the bottom of the track on that turn.

Tracey's palms were sweating inside her driving gloves. How much longer would she have to wait? The adrenaline was coursing through her body. She was ready to drive the race of her life. This was her moment to grasp her dream. But what about Rick? How was he feeling? To drive on the very track that had almost ended his life—

"Gentlemen, start your engines," the voice came over the loudspeaker.

Tracey almost giggled. They hadn't changed the traditional starting message, even though she certainly wasn't a "gentleman." She pressed the button on the dashboard that fired the engine into life.

The pace car came out and started to slowly lead the cars around the first lap. Like the other drivers, Tracey jerked the steering wheel right and then left to loosen up the car. It felt good. The car was handling just right—instantly responding to her movements.

Once they approached the starting point again, the cars were in their original formation. The green flag waved twice and the race was on.

Tracey shifted gears rapidly and revved up to almost one-hundred-fifty miles per hour in sixty seconds.

"Tracey, back off on the turns," Troy voice came over the earphones in her helmet. "Your tires are too cold to take them at full speed."

"Gotcha."

"How are you doing?"

"God, I can't believe how close they're driving. Fielding is only about five inches from me—we're going to trade paint if he gets any closer."

"Take it easy. He likes to jockey around—you know that. Don't let him intimidate you."

"Where am I standing?"

"Top ten—just settle in."

"Who's leading?"

Pause. "Rick."

Rick's speed had climbed almost to one-eighty as he pulled ahead of the pack. If he could drive this fast with his fuel tanks full, he could pick up speed as the tanks emptied and the car grew lighter.

"Talk to me, Rick," Skid's voice broke in on the earphones. "What's going on?"

"Feels good, Skid. What's my time?"

"You're about ten seconds in the lead—Carrera is right behind you. Not gaining though."

Rick was silent.

"Tracey Danvers is number six," Skid offered in a resigned voice. "But Fielding seems to be crowding her a little—he likes to rub rookies."

Tiny alarms bells went off in Rick's mind.

"Relax. She's handling it okay. In fact, she's a damn good driver." Skid sounded impressed.

"I'm going to try to get one lap ahead before we have to pit."

"Good. You're warmed up enough now—let it rip."

Tracey turned the wheel to the right and then left, trying to get around Fielding.

"Tracey, pull away from Fielding. He's not driving a calculated race. He's driving like a kamikaze pilot." Troy's voice was concerned.

"Can't. His car is slower and he's in the inside lane."

"Try passing on the outside after you get past the next turn."

"The outside?" Tracey exclaimed in surprise. Passing on the outside was always a gamble, because the other driver could force the passing car against the wall. "Are you sure?"

"Do it."

Tracey pulled around to the outside lane—a move Fielding obviously wasn't expecting. She shot around him, just as he tried to pull to the right and force her against the wall. Instead, he hit the wall and started to spin out.

"Great move!" Rick heard Skid shout in the microphone.

"What?"

"Your girl, Tracey, just slipped past Fielding and he went into the wall."

Rick smiled in satisfaction. Fielding was taking too many chances and that could cost other drivers their lives. While Rick didn't like seeing him out of the race so early, he felt better knowing he couldn't crowd Tracey again.

"Rick, watch it. Fielding's car is smoking and he's still up against the wall at turn four. The caution flag isn't out yet, so you're going to have to get past him," Skid warned. "Take the turn low."

Rick fought the rising panic as he approached the turn. Smoke billowed across the track, making it impossible for him to see—he had to trust Skid. As he steered low on the turn, he could hear the sounds of his former crash in his head. Sweat poured down the back of his neck—he started to brake. He had to run through it. He pressed down on the accelerator and held his breath. He shot through.

Once he cleared the smoke and the wreck, Rick clenched his fist in triumph. He had done it. It was almost like steering through the wreck of his own past when he shot through the smoke.

"Rick, are you all right?" Skid shouted into the microphone.

"The caution flag is out. I'm coming in to pit." Rick exhaled a long sigh of relief. Somehow the old ghosts seemed laid to rest.

Rick pulled the car into the pit area. His crew then sprang into action, refueling the tank and changing the tires with lightning speed.

"Move it. Move it," Skid shouted. "Get him back out there."

Rick pulled out as Tracey pulled into the pit area.

"Tires are good. Let's refuel," James Danvers yelled. "Come on. Come on. Get it moving."

Tracey shifted the car into gear and was back out on the raceway. She quickly resumed her position behind the pace car that had come out during the caution flag.

"One more lap—then the pace car ducks out. Get ready to jump your speed," Troy said tersely.

Tracey slammed down the accelerator as the green flag came out once more and the pace car moved off the track.

"What's my standing?" Tracey inquired after a few more laps.

"Third. You're through sixty laps," Troy answered.

"Whose ahead of me?"

"Rick's in first place by about thirty seconds. Then Carrera is only about ten seconds ahead of you."

"What's my time?"

"You're gaining."

"What about Rick?"

"He's slowed down a bit—seems to have settled in."

Skid's voice sounded worried. "Rick, Carrera is gaining on you—he's going to make his move soon."

"Outside or inside?"

"Can't tell, but Tracey's right on his tail. Could be tricky if she inadvertently blocks him."

"She can handle it, Skid." Rick hoped he sounded more certain than he really felt. Careful, Tracey, he thought.

"Rick, he's riding in your draft pull—he'll try to slingshot around you after you clear the next turn."

"I'm ready."

"Tracey, watch it," Troy warned. "I think Carrera is going to try to slingshot around Rick on the outside."

Tracey saw Paco make his move. Unthinkingly, she quickly steered to the right to block him. Just at that moment, Paco tried to swerve around Rick.

Their wheels brushed, and Tracey started to spin out.

"Steer into the spin." Tracey heard Troy in her mind before he even said it. "Hold it. Pull it straight again. Watch the wall—you're getting close."

Tracey's arm muscles strained tight with the effort of holding onto the vibrating steering wheel. The car was still spinning, but slowing down in momentum.

"I think I've got it back, Troy—" The jolt of another car hitting her right side sent her spinning again. This time her front end hit the wall.

The impact jerked Tracey forward.

"Damn it!" Troy shouted.

"I'm okay," Tracey said in a shaky voice. The car

scraped along the wall and eventually came to a halt. "I'm coming in."

As Tracey brought the car in, she felt a numbness in the pit of her stomach. The car was pulling to the right, the acceleration sluggish. She realized that the impact with the wall must have bent the front end— that meant transmission damage.

When she reached the pit area, Troy quickly scrambled under the front of the car.

Seconds later, one look at his face told her it was over.

"Sorry, Tracey, the front end is gone. You can't continue the race." Troy pulled the protective grate off the window and helped Tracey out of the car. He hugged her wordlessly for a few moments.

Tracey slowly pulled her helmet off, her head bowed in disappointment. She took deep breaths until she was strong enough to raise her head. "I thought I'd at least get to finish the race."

Troy squeezed her arm in reassurance. "You gave it your best shot."

Another car came roaring into the pit area behind them.

"Tracey!"

She whirled around at the sound of Rick's voice.

"Get in my car."

Chapter Eleven

"What?" Tracey stared at him incredulously.

Rick heard Skid's voice shouting in his headset: "What are you doing?" Rick whipped his helmet off. "Get in my car and finish the race."

"Rick, I can't—"

"Yes, you can. I want you to do it," Rick urged. "Look, there isn't much time—you've got to get back in the race before the caution flag lifts. Come on, Tracey."

Tracey hesitated. "But you've got to finish the race—"

Rick smiled. "I finished when I came through turn four. All my ghosts are gone."

Tracey shook her head. "No, I can't—"

Rick gripped her arms. "You're getting in that car if I have to pick you up and throw you in."

"But Rick, the sponsors—"

"All the sponsors care about is that their car finishes the race—it will, with you as driver."

Tracey glanced at Troy, hoping for guidance. He just shrugged.

"Get in the car, Tracey," Rick's voice rang out. "You've only got seconds!"

"Rick, why—"

His hands moved to cradle both sides of her face. A strange, eager look flashed in his eyes. "Finish the race." His lips came down on hers in a quick, searing kiss. "Finish it for both of us."

"I—" She was so confused, she couldn't speak.

"Tracey, get in the car!"

The seconds ticked away. Tracey finally nodded her head in a jerking motion. "Okay, I'll do it."

Rick grabbed her hand. They ran to his Grand Prix and he helped her in. The crowd roared as they watched Tracey slide into Rick's car.

Tracey jammed her helmet on. Rick's fingers flew as he snapped in the window grid. "Hurry! You've got about five seconds to get in front of the pace car—otherwise you'll be down one lap."

Tracey's eyes met his. "Thanks, Rick."

"Just get out there."

She pressed down on the accelerator and zoomed out onto the track, just ahead of the pace car.

"Have you lost your mind?" Skid asked as he caught up with Rick.

"I know what I'm doing—she's going to have her chance," Rick answered, his chin set resolutely. "Don't worry, all the sponsors care about is that the car finishes the race."

Skid shook his head in bafflement. "What about you?"

"I don't need it now." Rick watched Tracey maneuver his Grand Prix around the raceway, steadily gaining on the cars in the front pack. That driving need that had been pushing him was gone—he felt a deep contentment just watching Tracey achieve her dream.

He could no longer deny it. He loved her. When he had seen her spin out, he knew he couldn't let her drop out of the race. He had already won his own race.

"Rick, you take these," Troy offered as he held out his headset. "Tracey can use your experience."

Rick slipped Troy's headset on. "Tracey, are you there?"

Tracey felt a flood of pleasure run through her at the sound of Rick's voice. "I'm here. What's my standing?"

Rick watched the blur of cars moving around the track. "You're third again. There's one car between you and Carrera."

"How many laps to go?"

"About twenty. Don't overrev the engine—it's been pushed pretty hard. Just keep it steady."

"Okay. The car is feeling really loose," Tracey added using all her strength to hold the wheel steady. "It's hard to keep it on a straight line."

Rick gave a short laugh. "That's because it's balanced for my weight. You're a few pounds under."

Tracey answered with her own soft laugh. "I hope so."

Troy leaned over and showed Rick his stopwatch with the times of the second place car. "The car in front of you is slowing down, Tracey. After turn three, make your move and pass on the inside," Rick suggested tersely.

Tracey steered through the turn, taking it low. Then

she made a run at the car in front of her. She charged down the main straight, swerving to the left and then overtaking the car.

"I did it!" she shouted in elation. Her pulse was pounding. She was only one car away from the lead.

"Great driving, Tracey," Rick enthused.

"How far ahead is Paco?" she asked.

Rick paused. "About ten seconds."

"How many laps to go?"

"Ten."

Tracey swallowed hard. She couldn't gain on that lead unless Paco blew his engine or cut down a tire. But she could still give a spectacular finish. "I'm going to make a run on Paco."

"Be careful, Tracey, he'll push you into the wall if he thinks you're crowding him," Rick warned.

"I won't get closer than six inches."

"That's not much. He could get in a little deep and spin out. He'd take you with him." Rick watched her edge closer to Paco. He knew Paco would take her out if she threatened to get the drop on him. Paco would be merciless. He desperately wanted this win.

"I'm playing it careful, but I'm going to make a run at him." Tracey charged forward toward Paco's car.

"You're coming down to the final lap, Tracey. Don't crowd him." Rick was becoming increasingly uneasy as Tracey closed in on Paco's rear bumper.

"Rick, I can do it, but he's moving all over the track—blocking me," Tracey exclaimed.

"You're coming up to the final straight—just come in clean," Rick urged.

"I'm going to try the outside on a turn," she protested.

"NO!" Rick almost yelled. "Tracey, that's how I crashed eight years ago. It's a foolhardy move—not one worth your life." Rick took a deep breath. "I love you too much to see you take that kind of chance."

Something clicked in Tracey's mind. She backed off of Paco's bumper. She suddenly realized what Rick had been trying to tell her. She'd have a lot of races to run only if she played it smart—knowing each race wasn't the end. And that there was always something more important than winning—like Rick's love.

Paco roared past the finish line with Tracey right behind him.

"Tracey! You did it!" James Danvers threw his arms around his daughter. Lifting her off the ground, he spun her around. "I'm so proud. You ran a great race."

Tracey was laughing and crying all at once. Tears of joy made grooves through the grease and soot which covered the lower part of her face.

"Yeah! Tracey!" Troy chimed in. His arms stretched around both his father and sister. "You drove like a pro."

A shadow crossed her face. "You think I did the right thing? Backing off of Paco?"

"No doubt about it," Troy answered with complete conviction. "You lost too much time when you traded cars with Rick. This way you came in a clean second. You'll get a lot of points for that finish—and some dollars."

Mentioning Rick's car suddenly made her look around the pit area. "Where's Rick?"

Troy's gaze travelled over to the pit area where Rick's crew was located. "I don't see him with his pit crew."

"What Rick did for you today, no other man would do, Tracey," her father pointed out. "He's one in a million."

"I know, Dad." Tracey's eyes misted over, remembering Rick's declaration of love during the race. But did he mean it? she suddenly wondered. Or was it a way to get her to see the senselessness of her pushing herself beyond the limits? He had to mean it. She felt his love surround her, guide her across the finish line when she most needed him.

"So what are you waiting for?" Troy asked.

Her expression was quizzical. "I don't know—"

"Go find him," her father prompted. His voice grew tender. "Winning at love is the most important kind of victory. I guess I forgot that. Your mother would've reminded me."

Tracey nodded.

"You've got to have more in your life than racing cars," he added.

"I've had no regrets, Dad," Tracey said, struggling with her emotions. "This has been the greatest day of my life."

"Come on, let's not get mushy." Troy rolled his eyes in exasperation. "I'm going over to Victory Lane to see Paco—he drove a clean race and deserves it."

Tracey nodded in agreement. "Congratulate him for me, okay?"

"You got it—just make sure there's a job for me with Rick's crew, will you, Tracey?" he asked with a wink.

"Troy Danvers, I don't know what you mean." Tracey's cheeks grew warm with embarrassment. She dared not think about her future with Rick.

"Ignore your brother." Her father leaned over and kissed her on the forehead.

As she watched them stroll over to Victory Lane, Tracey felt a pang as she realized it would no longer be the three of them—the Danvers team. She was going off in a new direction, one that would take her away from them. They would still be a part of her life, but now she wanted other things as well. The things that Rick could offer her. At least, she hoped so. He had disappeared with his car after the race. Maybe he was regretting what he had done.

Where was he?

Tracey thought for a moment. She smiled. She knew where he had gone.

Jake's garage was empty when she arrived there. Everyone was still at the raceway—except one person.

"Rick?" she asked softly. He was leaning against the roof of his Grand Prix, his head down.

Rick looked briefly over his shoulder and then turned back to his car. Tracey felt small warning waves shoot through her—he didn't seem glad to see her at all.

"What are you doing here?" she inquired, almost afraid to ask.

Rick continued to look at the car in silence. Finally, he straightened up and turned his grey eyes on her. She gasped at the trace of sadness she found there. Her heart plummeted. This was it. He was going to give her the brush off.

"I came to say good-bye," Rick finally said.

A tremor of wild grief slashed through her. He was going to leave and never see her again. "I guess that's it then," she responded in an unsteady voice.

"Not completely."

"Oh, right, we'll still see each other at races. Looking at each other through the crowd," Tracey grated out bitterly. "You called me a coward, and now you're the one just taking off."

Rick eyes flashed genuine surprise. "What are you talking about?"

"You. Leaving. Saying good-bye. Fine, go. All that stuff you said during the race then was a big lie to get me to slow down," she accused. She knew she was making a fool of herself and she didn't care. She wasn't going to let Rick walk out of her life without a fight.

Rick stepped forward. "That wasn't a lie. I do love you. More than I ever dreamed it possible to love a woman."

Tracey's heart had started to clamor hopefully. "Then, what's this good-bye stuff?"

Rick moved closer, his hands reaching out to grasp Tracey's shoulders. "I was saying good-bye to a dream. It's hard. I've had that dream for eight long years. All that time I thought I wanted to come back and drive the Daytona. And I did."

"But you didn't finish." Tracey felt lost in the tenderness of his glance. "You let me finish instead."

Rick's arms slid around her, their faces almost touching. "That's because my dream was an illusion. I found the real thing—you."

"Rick—"

He cut her off as he placed a finger lightly over her lips. "I knew from that first day at the track you'd change my life forever—and you did. It isn't just your beauty—your green eyes that I could get lost in—it's you. Your courage. Your zest for life. I couldn't stay away. I had to drive in the rally with you just to be near you."

"And I thought you coveted my car," Tracey murmured against his finger.

"That, too," he teased.

Tracey bit him in playful response.

"Ouch." He snatched his hand away. "I couldn't stay away. Being in that car with you was sweet agony. We were together—but the Daytona kept us apart."

"No more. Rick, I love you so much," Tracey said joyfully. She felt tears of happiness fill her eyes as she threw her arms around his neck. She buried her face in his shoulder. He held her tightly, softly stroking her hair. Tracey surrendered to the protective haven of his embrace. This was where she belonged—forever.

Suddenly, she pulled back as a thought occurred to her. "Rick, does that mean you don't want to race anymore?"

Rick smiled into her eyes. "Sure I do—I just don't want to race against *you*. Too much tension."

Tracey felt a twinge of apprehension. "So what are we going to do?"

"That's what I was thinking about when you came in," Rick began, his voice growing meditative. "I was only driving again to prove something to myself. I did that. I'm not haunted by the race anymore, and I'm finished with drifting."

"But I didn't like being in engine design, because I was out of the excitement of the track," he continued. "So—"

"What?" Tracey resisted an impulse to shake it out of him.

"I'm going to open my own driving school. I liked teaching you while we were in the rally. I liked guiding you through the last laps of the Daytona. I've got a lot of knowledge I can pass on to rookie drivers—including you, Miss Danvers."

"Oh, Rick!" She hugged him hard. Then she pulled back. "Wait a minute. What do you mean 'teach me'? I can take care of myself, thank you."

"You would have blown the end of the Daytona if I hadn't calmed you down—"

"I would not . . . ," she trailed off, knowing he was right.

Rick gave her an inquiring look. "So what do you say? I'll manage and you drive?"

"On one condition." She played with the buttons on his shirt. "That I've got an option on starting a family in a few years."

Rick's eyes darkened with passion. His mouth came down on hers in a kiss that was a promise of all the love that they would share in the future. Tracey gave every part of herself, all her barriers down, feeling alive as she had never felt before. This was the race that they would both win.

"Rick, I've got to talk to you, man," Skid declared as he walked in on them.

Rick lifted his head reluctantly. "Skid, I'm a little busy right now."

Skid registered the couple locked in each other's arms. "Oh, great, you're both together," he continued, blithely unaware of their chagrin. "The race—I've got to talk to you, buddy."

"I did what I felt I had to—I hope you understand," Rick entreated in a calm voice. "Tracey needed—"

"Are you kidding?" Skid interrupted. "That was the greatest thing you could have done. Now listen, let me explain what I had in mind." He came up between them and put one arm around Tracey and the other around Rick.

"Uh-oh, Skid's on a roll," Rick tried to warn Tracey.

"Don't listen to him," Skid said with a dismissive tone. "We've got a gold mine here. Get it? This whole romance and race thing. We've got it sewn up. Rick Masters gives up his car so his love, Tracey Danvers, can finish the race. Can you imagine how the press will eat it up?"

Rick and Tracey exchanged glances of disbelief.

"Pictures, joint interviews. I'll set the whole thing up. What do you think?" Skid paused, waiting for their reaction.

"Skid," Rick tried to slow him down. "I'm thinking of starting my own driving school."

"Even better, even better. Racer/manager team—romance at the track."

"Rick, I think we'd better give in to the inevitable." Her lips were curved in a wry smile.

Rick nodded. "He's got us beat."

"Glad to hear you agree." Skid was practically singing with enthusiasm. "Now, first things first—"

"First, I'd like to finishing kissing Tracey," Rick answered firmly.

"Right. I understand. Just let me go out and get my camera, and we'll get a few pictures." He ran out of the garage.

Rick shook his head as Tracey started giggling.

"At least he approves," Tracey said between fits of laughter. "Quick, kiss me before he gets back with that camera."

Rick laughed and lowered his head to kiss her. He didn't need to be asked twice.